What the critics are saying...

℘

"Once again, Madison Hayes treats readers with a highly erotic, teasing, yet satisfying romance...*Dye's Kingdom: Wanting it Forever* is absolutely unforgettable." ~ *Fallen Angel Reviews*

"*Wanting it Forever* is wonderfully written with complex characters and a love that was meant to be. Clever, erotic, sensual and at times emotional, this book is a great addition to any reader's erotica library." ~ *Cupid's Library Reviews*

"*Dye's Kingdom: Wanting it Forever* is a fast-paced, tension-filled, sexually explosive story that you'll want to read again and again...*Ms. Hayes* creates an elaborate, intricate and intriguing world which will draw you in and keep you *Wanting it Forever*." ~ *Fallen Angel Reviews*

"*Dye's Kingdom: Wanting it Forever* is a fast paced story that pulled me into another world...*Madison Hayes* is a truly wonderful storyteller." ~ *Enchanted in Romance*

Madison Hayes

DYE'S KINGDOM: Wanting it Forever

ELLORA'S CAVE
ROMANTICA PUBLISHING

An Ellora's Cave Romantica Publication

www.ellorascave.com

Dye's Kingdom: Wanting it Forever

ISBN #1419952935
ALL RIGHTS RESERVED.
Dye's Kingdom: Wanting it Forever Copyright © 2005 Madison
Hayes
Edited by Pamela Campbell
Cover art by Syneca

Electronic book Publication May 2005
Trade paperback Publication November 2005

Warning:

The following material contains graphic sexual content meant for mature readers. This story has been rated E–rotic by a minimum of three independent reviewers.

Ellora's Cave Publishing offers three levels of Romantica™ reading entertainment: S (S-ensuous), E (E-rotic), and X (X-treme).

S-*ensuous* love scenes are explicit and leave nothing to the imagination.

E-*rotic* love scenes are explicit, leave nothing to the imagination, and are high in volume per the overall word count. In addition, some E-rated titles might contain fantasy material that some readers find objectionable, such as bondage, submission, same sex encounters, forced seductions, and so forth. E-rated titles are the most graphic titles we carry; it is common, for instance, for an author to use words such as "fucking", "cock", "pussy", and such within their work of literature.

X-*treme* titles differ from E-rated titles only in plot premise and storyline execution. Unlike E-rated titles, stories designated with the letter X tend to contain controversial subject matter not for the faint of heart.

Also by Madison Hayes

෨

Dyes Kingdom:
Wanting it Forever

Dedication

&

To Theseus...

Chapter One

"Who died and made you king?" With her upper lip curled into a sneer, Martigay snorted at the big man's back—then watched that back freeze in defensive disbelief. Slowly the man turned to face her, stunned incredulity stamped into his expression. The long, curving line of his lips parted as he stared, and Martigay was suddenly taken with the idea that...the large, intimidating man was...exceptionally...attractive.

Attractive in an undeniably hard, male sense, impossible to ignore and unlikely to be overlooked. His broad, square shoulders spanned the chest of a mountaineer, wide and deep, and a heavy wool cloak was pushed back over the wide line of those shoulders. The long sleeves of his linen jerkin were pushed up to his elbows, exposing tanned forearms touched with a burnish of fair hair and patterned with a strong network of veins. The frayed edge of his doeskins were cinched tight around a tapered waist and his plain, soft leggings bunched at his groin, then hugged his legs in loose folds to tuck into the top of scuffed leather boots. Her eyes lingered a moment at his groin before they made a reluctant departure and followed his long legs all the way to the ground.

In a cool appraisal, Martigay let her eyes slowly rise to his face. And that was where her dispassionate veneer failed her. The man was unmistakably first-class, grade-A, level one, hunk-quality material—nudged right up there next to godhood.

The man was...*dangerously* handsome. He looked like the sort of man who would kill for what he wanted and would kill again before giving it up. The hard planes of his face spoke of violent hours on the battlefield and threatened danger as well as promised protection. The lines that bracketed his hard mouth had probably never seen a smile. Imagining how it might feel to be possessed by such a man, a shiver went up Martigay's spine. As he glared at her, Martigay's eyes drifted to the dark tattoo slashing his left eyebrow.

Tattoos were uncommon in the men of her generation, though older men, especially Khals, sported intricate patterns that covered half their foreheads and extended downward across one eyelid. But this tattoo was a departure from the dark, scrolling artwork seen on older Khals. It was a simple, violent, arcing slash that cut from his hairline down through his eyebrow, ending just above his eye.

Tucked inside the shadowed hood of his cloak, loose strands of his hair shone as bright as the sun on oranges. With an irritated twitch of his head, the demigod flicked the straight hair out of his eyes as he narrowed his angry gaze on her. Those eyes blazed a virulent, volcanic blue from beneath the cold edge of a frown. "What's your rank, soldier?" His voice was a hard, dangerous scrape.

Abruptly, Martigay realized she may have blundered, and seriously. At her side, she heard Pall snuff out a gasp of startled amusement. She pushed her shoulders back. "What's it to you?"

Someone coughed in the still tavern and there was a scrape of wooden chair against stone floor along with the warning sizzle of meat blackening on the spit in the fireplace.

The man's hood slid from his head, revealing the three gold ribbons of rank braided into his hair and Martigay clamped her teeth in hard regret. *Damn*. When she'd entered the busy tavern and found the man upbraiding one of her comrades, she'd taken him for an arrogant, threadbare aristocrat of little consequence. With his hood covering his head, she couldn't have known he outranked her…and then some. Unwilling to acknowledge defeat, her jaw jutted forward.

"What's your rank?" he repeated, his words a cold command.

That command put a shiver down her backbone like ice shards driven into her spine. With a blink, she straightened, irritated that the officer would ask what he could clearly see braided into her hair.

"Field Captain, Commander," she announced with all the professional snap she could muster. There was a moment's silence, and though she didn't watch those burning eyes, she felt them bore right through her, all the way to her spine.

"Not anymore." His voice was a harsh, contained rasp, like steel against steel. "Pawyn."

Martigay winced. She knew she'd winced and it had shown, though she'd preferred to have hidden it. "As you say, Commander."

His hand was extended toward her, palm up.

Quickly, she reached for the blue ribbon in her hair and tugged at the knot with two fingers. Her hand hovered above his a defiant moment before she loosed the ribbon and watched it fall into his hand.

Slouching back against the counter — the casual act meant to punctuate her façade of indifference — she boldly settled her eyes on his, as the two of them exchanged their mutual disdain. At some point, the man's eyes fired in response to her impertinence — the soldier's complete absence of deference or concern apparently moving the officer to further action.

"Report to my tent tomorrow, after firstmeal," he delivered curtly. With that, the commander motioned to his two attendants as he pushed through the tables and out of the tavern.

And it wasn't until then that she even realized the entire clientele and every soldier within the tavern, with the possible exception of Pall, was holding his or her collective breath. Every set of eyes was fixed on her.

With a careless smirk, she shrugged, lifting her shoulders. "What?" she complained to Pall as she turned back to the counter signaling for a jack of ale. "The man was an arrogant son of a marmot — picking on poor Wags like that!"

She grinned up at the man behind the counter, expecting him to confirm this opinion with nothing less than a nod. Instead, the barkeep stared at her as if she were mad.

"Wags is hard on his mount," Pall reminded her lightly. "His *army* mount. You, yourself, have complained about it."

Martigay lifted a shoulder. "Still, the commander needn't have to come down on me! I was only sticking up for a man in my unit. I didn't know he was an officer." The barkeep slid a jack of ale before her and she took a long swallow. "He might have considered that! The man has no sense of humor," she finished dismissively.

Elbows on the counter, Pall nodded agreeably and turned his face to hers. His green gaze was filled with barely suppressed amusement as he looked out at her through a curtain of straw-colored hair. "You might be short on humor, too, if your grandmother—The Queen—had died last month."

Martigay stared at him with dawning horror.

"I understand our new king was very close to the old lady."

* * * * *

Several ales afterward, Martigay staggered against Pall as they reeled their way through camp, coming to an unsteady halt just outside his tiny camp tent. Catching her arm, Pall only just stopped her teetering descent to the ground. "Come on, then," he grinned down at her, eyes laughing out of a tanned face. "Give us a shag?"

She nodded several times. "Sounds good to me."

Pall laughed. "And in the morning—will you still respect me?"

"Don't respect you now," she pointed out. "Don't see any reason to change my opinion."

Pall considered this statement for a few moments before formulating his reply. "Promise you'll not kill me and we'll call it a deal."

Scrunching her face up in concentration, she gave this idea some thought. "Can't guarantee that," she admitted.

With a grin and an arm around her, Pall pushed her along to her tent that had been pitched just beyond his. Hers was slightly larger, with room enough for two people to sleep and high enough to sit in without mussing your hair on the tent's roof. Tucking her inside, Pall crawled in behind her and helped her struggle with her uncooperative bedding. When she was covered and settled, he scuttled backward to leave.

"I deserved that field promotion," she slurred.

"Is that a rhetorical statement?"

"Mmph?"

"Do you expect a response?"

"Bastard."

"Who? The new king or me?"

"The king. Effing, royal bastard. Bet he's never done anything more taxing in his life than lift a golden goblet to his mouth. Bet he needs help getting undressed. Bet he's white as a slug under those doeskins," she grumbled disingenuously, flashing on the image of the king's lean, tawny forearms, "and as soft as a —

"*I'm sorry,*" she announced loudly to the tent's roof, and Pall heard her teeth grate in the next quiet instant. "I didn't *know* who he was, didn't *know* he'd lost his grandmother!

"When did he get here?" she complained. "Why didn't you tell me *the king* would be commanding the army?" Martigay sighed. "I deserved that promotion, Palleden."

Pall nodded. She had. Deserved it, and earned it.

The river crossing shouldn't have been a problem, earlier that day, even though the water was high. But one of the oxen had floundered on the slippery pavers and had gone down. The tall, bulky wagon had started downstream, dragging the tangled harness and both oxen with it. Men had hurried toward the wagon, sloshing clumsily through the water as the wagon began to roll and tip.

Helplessly, they'd watched as the large mass moved away faster than they could catch it up.

Then they'd watched Martigay slash across the river several paces downstream.

She'd knotted her rope low on a tree at the bank's edge and charged her pony into the rush of water. Urging her mount up the cobbled bank on the opposite side of the river, she jumped from her horse and wrapped the rope's end around a second tree. The rope stretched taut as the wagon glided to meet it.

The rope had halted the wagon long enough for many strong hands to get behind it. The oxen were cut free to flounder their way to the bank while others from her unit heaved the wagon to shore. Pall nodded. There was no question that Martigay had earned the blue ribbon the king had demanded she return.

Pall shook his head regretfully. That promotion had meant a lot to her. She was ambitious. It had taken months of hard, perspiring application for her to work her way from pawyn to sergeant. Then in a day she was captain.

And that had lasted exactly one day.

The king needn't have busted her all the way down to pawyn. He could have stopped at sergeant.

Still, Pall thought, his mouth lifting at one corner, the girl's spirit didn't appear to be broken.

"Arrogant, overbearing, pompous, royal little prick. Born with a silver...place setting...in his mouth." She halted on these last words, stumbling over the visual image of the king's hard, sensuous lips, his hair slicked away from his face and hanging down in a straight sheet to touch the wide line of his shoulders. Sweeping this idea aside with a brush of impatience, she looked to Pall to confirm her opinion. "Where'd he come from anyway?"

Pall shrugged. "Don't know much about him. From what I've heard, he wasn't exactly next in line for the crown. The Queen bypassed quite a lot of family to put him on the throne."

"Wonder who he bullied, intimidated, bribed and murdered to assure his ascension," she mumbled morosely.

Pall smiled down into her smoke-blue eyes and let his gaze drift from there. Most men didn't even get as far as her eyes, he knew. Most men never got past her beautifully rounded breasts—when she was facing them. And when she wasn't facing them, it was her luscious, curving hips and trim little bottom.

"He'll be sorry he ever crossed steel with me." She swaggered with bravado. "I'll make him pay for this…in gold. I'll be a lieutenant before I'm finished with the King of Thrall. And I'll be wearing a gold ribbon in my hair."

"I've no doubt you will," Pall told her consolingly as his eyes were drawn to the dark waves that haloed her head. "Why do you rub henweed into your hair?" he asked. "It's a beautiful color." It was. A rich, vibrant red so dark it had purple undertones.

"That's why I rub henweed into it, silly."

"I've never seen anything like it before. What would it be otherwise—without the color?"

"Not so red," she muttered up at the ceiling.

He put a pat on her knee. "Check on you in the dawning, then."

Her fist made its wavering way to her forehead. "G'nite, Sergeant," she slurred with gloomy resignation.

Pall hesitated at the tent's opening. "Be careful, Martigay. You made a powerful enemy today."

Martigay rolled her eyes upward. "You must be mistaken, Pall," she drawled. "I'm too lazy to make enemies." Pall smiled as he left. There were a lot of words to describe Martigay—but lazy wasn't one of them.

* * * * *

Not a hundred paces distant, Dye stretched back in his camp chair, his eyes on the roof of his pavilion tent. The table before him was littered with stacks of ledgers, sheaves of correspondence and piles of curled-up maps. He shook his head.

He couldn't let a soldier get away with that sort of disrespect. The girl had to be disciplined. As the new king taking over command of the Army, he couldn't afford to start off on weak footing. He should have dismissed the woman. Normally, he would have. If it had been a man, he probably would have. But at the time, he hadn't been able to bring himself to the act. There was something about the girl that couldn't be easily dismissed. Impertinent little—but the soldier probably hadn't realized whom she was addressing when she'd made the awkward statement...and it might turn out better this way, he decided. It would give him an opportunity to make an example of the soldier.

He shook his head again, but it wasn't in regret or disagreement. It was a physical effort to shake his mind free of the cocky, arrogant little face that had been following him around all evening. That was with him now, as he stared at the tent's ceiling.

His hand raked back through his red hair before it dropped into his lap. Unconsciously, his thick wrist scraped over the ties that laced his doeskin leggings together at the groin.

It had been a crap fucking month, starting with the unexpected call to Gluthra—royal seat of Greater Thrall—where his grandmother had lived and ruled for almost eighty years. Dye was only one of the Old Queen's many grandchildren who'd gathered after the old lady's death.

He'd gone to attend the firing of her funeral pyre and to see his sister step up to lead the country. But Petra had unexpectedly declined the throne, and instead of a new queen, Thrall had gotten a new king. No one had been more surprised than he to learn that his name was listed as second in line for the throne. It's not as if he, or Petra for that matter, was the oldest of Tien's grandchildren or even born to her oldest offspring.

Within days, his leadership had been challenged, not by any of his cousins—they were smarter than that—but by a distant challenge in the tiny, prosperous country of Amdahl and part of his Kingdom. The desert clans of the Saharat had pulled together and invaded their tiny eastern neighbor. As the smallest country in the considerable collection known as Greater Thrall or Thrall & Etc., the small city-state had been overrun in a matter of days. No doubt the Saharat had felt the timing was right to invest in the attractive oceanside property while leadership was changing hands in far-off Gluthra, located north across the middle sea—with several days of ocean and the whole length of Agryppa to cross before help could reach Amdahl.

And that, thought Dye, was the reason he was presently camped a day's ride south of Tharran, the Agryppan capitol, on his way to Amdahl with an army of twelve thousand.

To take back Amdahl. With ten thousand from Thrall—including the two thousand small, pale men indigenous to the country, and after whom the country was named—as well as two thousand from Agryppa. Not because Greater Thrall needed the income generated by the bustling port city, but because the people of Amdahl were used to the freedom that came with being part of Thrall & Etc. And because they expected the protection and assistance they'd requested.

Sending his army on ahead, under the command of his Senior Lieutenant, he'd only just caught up with his men. Normally, he'd have accompanied his army, despite their slow rate of travel, but complications at home had kept him from setting out with his troops.

Dye sighed. At the same time he'd received Amdahl's request for help, there had been rumblings and threats from Vandaland in the north. He snorted. No surprise there. Damn Vandals.

Well aware of the dangers involved in fighting battles on two separate fronts, he'd bought the Vandals off with a contract.

A shrewd move on his part. One that might finally put an end to a hundred years of animosity, not to mention at least a thousand deaths every year—those deaths the result of border skirmishes for which the Vandals were largely to blame. He'd drawn up the contract himself, and signed it. Dye shrugged. The yellow-haired Vandal princess was nice enough to look at. She'd make as good a wife as any other woman.

Nodding to himself, he stared at the canvas ceiling then shook his head again, palming the front of his leggings as he did so.

Chapter Two

The king's tent was silent as Martigay was ushered through the opening, stopping just inside. He was seated at the head of a long, light, folding table, his many officers filling out the sides. Saluting him with a closed fist, Martigay awaited his command.

Leaning back in his chair, Dye gave the pawyn a long, appraising stare. "Thank you for reporting, soldier. I have a task that requires some special talent…and you came immediately to mind." At that, he paused. "I would have my boots cleaned."

She felt—actually felt—red anger climb her neck and paint her cheeks. "Yes, sir," she answered. Scanning the room, she located a shining pair of boots next to a closed trunk.

"With your tongue."

Martigay's eyes closed to slits as her head tilted and she regarded the King of Thrall. Then she was moving. A few rapid steps moved her around the thick tent post supporting the pavilion and placed her before the king. Dropping to her knees, she pushed his knees apart. Her angry eyes connected with his for an instant before she lowered her head between his legs and put her tongue on top of his knee-high boots.

"Not these boots!"

She raised her head. "I'm sorry, sir," she said, but it sounded more like a threat than an apology.

"The black pair, there against the trunk."

She didn't move. "But, My Lord. The black pair is clean. Here is where my tongue will be most useful. If his Lordship would just *spread his knees*," she grated as she jabbed her elbows against the inside of his thighs, "I'll give these the licking they deserve!"

Behind her, she heard a muffled whine of suppressed laughter and glanced up to see Dye glare across the table at one of his lieutenants.

"Why," he almost shouted, "do you have *so* much trouble following orders, soldier? I would have the black boots polished."

Her fingers tightened to clutch the muscles above his knees as she pushed herself up and away. "As you say, sir." Crossing the room, Martigay swept one of the boots from the floor. Ten officers watched her tongue lick out of her mouth as she nestled the boot between her fabulous breasts.

"Continue your report, Marcan," Dye ordered as his patience began to fray.

But all ten of the king's officers were staring at the woman who stood behind their leader. Small moans of pleasure issued from her throat as she ran her tongue down the long, glistening surface of the shining boot.

Dye's shoulders knotted as he squeezed his eyes tightly shut. When he opened them again, he found his youngest lieutenant slack-jawed and staring beyond his left shoulder. "Marcan! Your report."

His lieutenant shook himself and continued his report in a distracted monotone, his attention fixed elsewhere. And Dye knew exactly where his attention was fixed. Dye's fist tightened as the girl's moans and sighs increased in volume. In the middle of Marcan's broken monologue, he stood abruptly and whipped around to face his pawyn. "Thank you, soldier. That will do."

Slowly, Martigay leaned over to return the boot to the ground. The low scoop of her simple jerkin fell open and every man on the left side of the table craned forward to watch her descent. She straightened with a sharp snap, suddenly the soldier again. "Yes, sir. Anything else you want cleaned, sir?"

His fists bunched at his sides and he shook his head. "You're dis*missed*," he gritted out in three separate syllables.

Her stance relaxed as she began her sauntering exit. "No? Sure you don't want your bollocks polished? Your testes tasted?" She threw him a final arch look. "Let me know if you have any further use for my...talents," she suggested just before she disappeared through the open flaps of the tent.

As Dye stood staring at the tent's exit, several of his lieutenants coughed loudly, their hands covering their mouths and their eyebrows pinched together. With his knuckle, Lieutenant Greegor wiped at the corner of one eye as Dye dropped back into his chair. For a long time he just stared at the door while his lieutenants caught their breaths.

At last, his most senior officer, Lieutenant Greegor, spoke up. "If she can do that to a man's boots—with her tongue...I wonder what she might do...with a little polish." His voice trailed away as he caught the king's expression.

Lieutenant Marcan, like the king, still stared at the door. Having missed the king's expression, he cleared his throat. "Do you suppose she likes flowers?"

Greegor nodded. "If you're thinking to impress the young woman, the way to that girl's heart is through her horse," he volunteered. "What's she call him?"

"Scarface."

Dye's eyes swung around to the officer who had named her mount. "Lieutenant Prithan. Has she been a discipline problem before?"

"Sir!" The man seemed surprised by the question. "She's in my unit. Captain...Pawyn Martigay has never been any kind of a problem. She's hard-working, dedicated, very ambitious, sir."

"Ambitious." The king's word hung there in the air and everyone understood its meaning. "How ambitious?"

Quickly, the officer shook his head. "Not like that, sir. Not at all. At least," the man smiled, "I never got that lucky." Lieutenant Prithan glanced around the table, almost furtively. Most of the men were smiling but giving nothing away.

"Gentlemen?" the king inquired in a soft, edgy voice.

21

One by one, each man shook his head.

"Is that a problem, sir?" one of his officers ventured carefully, "because there's a woman in the archers and we…"

"Your relationships are your own business," the king said shortly. "But they shouldn't be mixed with a soldier's advancement. Make sure you keep your personal relationships separate from your work."

"Thank you, sir." The officer hesitated before continuing. "Sir, several of the women have expressed an interest in…meeting you, sir."

"I'll remind you I'm to be wed to the Princess Bruthinia," he said in a voice like ice floes locking. "We'll leave it at that."

* * * * *

Martigay whistled—two short bursts and one long. From a distance came an answering whinny. Moments later a small paint stallion was cantering through camp, weaving through the tents toward his mistress. Martigay rubbed his nose with her closed fist, teasing him with the oats she held wrapped inside her small hand. "Hey boy," she murmured. "Check out the new little gray?"

Scarface threw his head with a snort, nosing at her fist.

"What?! What's wrong with her?" Martigay turned to where the mare stood. "So she's got a spotty ass. Like you're such a prize." She slapped the paint's rump. "She's just your size."

The paint nudged his head against Martigay's face, took hold of her braid and tugged it as he backed up a few steps.

"Stop that," she chided as the horse pulled her face around. "Oh," she said, staring at a long, leggy bay. "Well, you're ambitious, aren't you?" She cocked her head. "Dresses a bit sluttishly, don't you think?"

Letting go of the braid, the horse swung his head vigorously.

Martigay sighed. "You're right. It's a beautiful saddle." Wistfully, she gazed at the ruddy leather harness that must have cost at least five gold. Curling scrolls of silver were inset on the saddlebow. "You'd look good in it, boy. It'd match your eyes perfectly." Opening her hand, she let her horse pick the grain out of her palm. "Well, good luck with the mare, Scarface. But I'm warning you, if you want that one, you're going to have to bring her to her knees...just to mount her."

A flash of light at the king's tent drew her attention, just as Pall scuffed across the clearing to join her.

Half of the king's Royal Guard, traditionally made up of Thralls, was reporting for duty. Twenty-five of the small, pale men marched to their station, pink eyes fixed in the chalk-white of their faces. The Thralls' captain marched separately from the guards' ranks and, as he moved, the light was caught and reflected on the many gold bands he wore on his long arms.

Pall looked at Martigay, her eyes fixed across the clearing. His gaze followed hers to the king's tent. "What's up?" he asked, as Dye ducked out of the tent.

"Why does the king keep a Thrallish guard?" Martigay asked, her eyes on the redhead.

"Tradition," Pall answered. "Morghan started it—to honor the people of Thrall." He shrugged. "Morghan was no fool. He must have looked like a giant when he was surrounded by his Thrallish guard."

"From what I've heard, Morghan would have been a giant next to any man."

"That's probably true," Pall agreed. "And it's not as though Morghan needed a guard. He could take on a small army alone, without breaking a sweat. On the other hand," Pall mused, "though Thralls aren't large, they're reliable if somewhat inflexible. They'll follow an order to the death." Pall smiled at Martigay, whose eyes were fixed on the tall red-haired king. Leaning toward her, he whispered in her ear, "You're staring."

She lifted her chin a fraction, in the king's direction. "Those doeskins appear to have seen rough trade. You'd think the king could afford a new pair."

"You'd think so," Pall agreed.

"Wonder what he's got under those leggings."

"Martigay! If you need a man, I'll be more than happy to—"

She snorted in response, squinting at the king as he shared a few words with his captain. "Do you think that was a smile?" she asked Palleden.

"Hard to say," he returned stingily, disinclined to encourage her interest in the king.

A slight breeze tugged at her hair. Absently, she pulled a few strands from her mouth as she watched the breeze riff through the king's straight mane of polished copper. As his hair moved, the sun put streaks of fire into the sheet of hair he wore pushed behind his ears.

"Wonder what that mouth looks like when it smiles."

"Thought you were mad at him."

"Furious," she answered absently. "I'd like to get him in bed. Show him a thing or two."

Pall fixed his eyes pointedly on her chest. "And you're just the girl for the job."

She laughed. "Going down to watch the race?"

"Maybe. How about you?"

"I'm in it."

"How fair is that?" Pall protested.

Martigay shrugged. "I'm giving the others a lead of fifty paces."

"You going to win?"

"You know Scarface."

Pall nodded. The little stallion couldn't bear for another horse to lead him. Reaching for his pouch, he clinked out several coins and then closed his fist on the handful of silver. "My money's on you, then," he said, backing away from her.

But her eyes had returned to the red-haired king.

"It's bent," he threw at her as he withdrew.

"What?"

"Rumor is — it's *bent*," he said again, grinning at her.

Martigay shook her head, her eyes narrowing on the retreating figure of her friend. Raising her shoulders, she shook her head at him. "What's bent?"

Pall motioned toward the king in the distance. "You wanted to know what he had under his doeskins," he reminded her with a laugh.

Martigay's jaw dropped suddenly as she slowly turned to stare at the king. Behind her, she heard the receding sound of Pall's amusement.

"Like a bow!" he chortled from a distance "Only, from what I understand, your hand would be a bit small for the grip."

Chapter Three

On the bluff above the valley, Dye pulled his mount to a stop as he frowned at the crowd of milling horses on the open floor below. "What's going on?" Twisting in his saddle, he put the question to his lieutenant, Greegor.

"Looks like a race, sir."

In the valley below, horses and men crowded and jostled together as the riders struggled to keep their impatient mounts pointed in the right direction. As Dye watched, there must have been some sort of signal because, all at once, the mass of riders surged forward toward the open end of the valley.

Turning his head, Dye watched as the clump separated out into leaders and followers. He didn't notice the paint at first. It certainly hadn't started with the lead. Halfway up the straight valley it caught his eye, eating up the distance that separated it from the pack of horses leading the race. At one point the track narrowed, pinched in by brush on both sides, and Dye held his breath as the beasts pushed through the bottleneck, bumping against one another. The paint alone veered from the path to fight its way through the low tangle of brush before it continued on to make two similar jumps. Dye watched with keen interest as the little horse screamed into the lead, its rider hunched forward over the pony's neck as it barreled ahead to reach the mouth of the canyon alone, the other riders trailing in its dust.

Dye smiled at his lieutenant. "How many messengers do I have?"

"Three, My Lord."

He pointed to the mouth of the canyon. "Is that rider one of them?"

The man squinted into the valley, opened his mouth, closed it, then opened it again. "I don't believe so, sir."

"Make that soldier Captain of my Messengers."

* * * * *

As Martigay breezed into the king's tent, the door's flaps were sucked up in her wake to follow her partway inside. Abruptly, she halted in mid-stride, leaning to stare past the wide tent post at the king, her eyes fastened on his bared chest. Impressive slabs of muscle shifted in his upper body as he turned toward her. A light covering of burnished hair glowed on the gold skin between his nipples, before it collected into a line and dove into the doeskin leggings that hung low on his hips.

His ties were undone, lank and loose like an unfinished story. A story that needed finishing. A story she'd like to finish. Slowly, the back of Martigay's wrist moved up to wipe her bottom lip as she gazed at the point at which the line of hair disappeared beneath the loose ties.

A deep bowl of water sat on the table before the king as he'd just finished scraping his chin. A few damp strands of hair hung over his forehead to shadow the dark tattoo slashing his left eyebrow. Martigay watched as water ran down the hard line of his jaw, dripped from the square of his chin and splashed to trail down the hard, granite lines of his chest.

The fine copper hair on his chest failed to hide a large scar that ripped from collarbone to breastbone while numerous smaller scars strafed shoulders and arms that were neither *soft* nor *white*.

"Soldier," he prompted her impatiently, then froze. "*What* is that blue ribbon doing back in your hair?" he inquired coldly. "And what are you doing here?"

"Sir. You asked me to report."

"I did nothing—" his eyes flicked to the blue ribbon in her hair. She hadn't been announced which meant...he'd sent for her.

"You ride a paint pony," he stated—gathering himself quickly. "Captain...Martigay. Thanks for reporting." Reaching around behind him he lifted a scroll from the table and held it toward her. "For Lieutenant Marcan. It's not urgent," he said after a moment's hesitation. "Skirt the mud flats if you must."

"The mud's not a problem, sir."

He nodded. "I'll expect you back before dusk, then. Check in with me on your return. Be care—keep your eyes open. Avoid any other riders you might see."

"Sir." She acknowledged this order with the professionalism of a soldier then delayed in her departure, halted by a very female curiosity. "Where'd you get that scar?" she asked, her eyes on his chest.

He stared at her for a moment. "This one?" His finger traced the thin white line that slashed across his chest as she nodded without speaking. "The civil war. In Khal."

"I...didn't think Thrall was involved in that conflict."

"It wasn't."

"Then what were you doing there?"

"I grew up in Khal. Fought for the North."

She nodded again, though her expression was still puzzled. "How about that one? There on your shoulder."

"I got that one on Earth."

"*Earth?* Is that an island?"

This question stopped him for a moment as he considered his answer. "In a manner of speaking," he finally agreed. Reaching for his jerkin, he pulled the linen shirt over his head. "But it's a long story, soldier," he told her dismissively.

In answer to this, Martigay hit her forehead with her fist and turned to leave.

"Two fingers, Martigay," he corrected her quietly.

Slowly she turned back to face him, eyes narrowed in daring challenge.

"Two fingers in *my army*, soldier."

There was more than a hint of arrogance in her slow smile. "Yes, sir. Which two would you have, sir…and where would you have them?"

Now the king's eyes narrowed at her impudence. His hand traveled slowly to his forehead as he demonstrated the two-finger salute for his new captain. Just as slowly, Martigay's fingers rose to her temple to snap off a salute, then dropped to her lips, where they lingered an instant, before tipping toward him. With a smart turn, Martigay was out of the tent.

Uncertainly, Dye stared at the tent's door. *Had his new Captain of Messengers just blown him a kiss?*

Unsmiling, he shook his head as he tugged at his ties and tried to loop them into a knot, his eyes still on the tent's exit. After several attempts, he looked down at the leather strings and realized his work was complicated by a rising tide of thickening flesh.

Falling back into his chair, he shook his head again — in frustration — as he drummed up the memory of the last woman he'd laid. Then the one before that and, when that didn't work, the one before that. But intruding into these memories was a saucy vixen with rich red hair, tan doeskins hugging the curves of her legs, her jerkin cut low on her chest and barely held closed with a thin twist of leather.

Like a spring uncoiling, Dye stood suddenly and bolted through the tent's opening.

His two guards followed him to the river, where he threw himself into the cold rush. Gasping, he surfaced in the icy stream, slicking his hair back and blinking the water out of his eyes before slogging his way slowly toward the bank, water sliding off his hair and down his shoulders as the river dragged at his legs.

He was just going to have to get wed, he thought. To Bruthinia of Vandaland. He would do well to remember that…whether he wanted to or not.

Chapter Four

Dye reined in his mount and glanced back over his shoulder. He'd noticed the wasps' nest clinging to the old bristlecone when he'd passed the ancient tree. Now he pulled his mount to a halt fifty paces beyond the tree. Reaching for his bow and stringing it, he motioned to Lieutenant Prithan, then waited for the lieutenant's unit to go by, pulling the girl out as she passed.

The woman was far too sure of herself for his liking and he'd been looking for an opportunity to bring her down a notch since the boot incident in his tent. As a commander, he knew the danger of impertinence and disrespect—knew its ability to destroy an army from within. And if the girl thought she was going to charm her way through the ranks by blowing kisses where a salute was appropriate—she had better start rethinking. It was time to put the soldier in her place.

The wasps' nest wasn't huge, probably housing no more than twenty or thirty of the nasty wee beasts, but he thought it would serve his purpose.

"Captain Martigay," he started, "Lieutenant Prithan and I have a wager going." He pointed to the wasps' nest in the distance.

Prithan's expression was one of surprise while the girl's was wary as she regarded the distant nest—a muddy, mottled blotch hugging a wide split in the old bristlecone.

Dye pulled an arrow from the quiver holster on his saddle. "You can judge the outcome of the contest for us. I'm to hit that wasps' nest to win." Drawing the bowstring tighter than was warranted, he let the arrow fly. There was a dull, distant thud as the arrowhead was driven through the nest and its head sank deep into the tree's trunk. Immediately, a cloud of dusty specks appeared to dip and hover about the pierced nest.

Dye looked at the girl.

"It was a large enough target," she pointed out.

He held her eye. "Damn," he delivered, coolly and unconvincingly. "I've just realized. That was my lucky arrow." The woman looked as though she'd been expecting exactly this, but waited for the order just the same. "Retrieve my arrow, soldier."

He caught just a flicker of fire in her eyes before she turned her pony's head and cantered easily in the direction of the tree. As she rode away, he caught sight of a long, saw-toothed scar running down the back of her arm. For some reason, the sight of that soft female curve, so viciously defaced, released an unanticipated flood of compassion for the girl. Immediately, he regretted his command. Clenching his teeth to keep from canceling his order, Dye wheeled his impatient mount as he watched her come level with the tree, but off to one side about twenty paces as she turned her horse to face the bristlecone.

Frowning at the distant figure, he wondered what she had in mind. He knew the arrow's shaft was set firmly in the tree's trunk and would take some wrestling to work free. As he watched, he saw her head toss, swore he saw her eyes slide toward him with a mean, metallic gleam of warning. He watched her lean over her pony's neck, her mouth close to the pony's ear—and the horse was off. He saw the little paint fly past the tree without slowing. Waiting for the paint to turn, he pulled at his reins as his horse tossed its head.

Twenty paces past the tree, the soldier pulled her mount into a wide turn and he looked for the arrow. She held it aloft in one hand and he cursed.

But it was a curse of relief—as well as pleasure.

Tearing across the ground toward him, the soldier reined her pony to a prancing halt before him. A swift glance at her face and arms assured him she was unharmed as he let out a breath he hadn't realized he was holding. Her leg swung over the back of her mount and she landed lightly on the ground before she took the few paces between them. She held the arrow forward in both hands, like an offering, and he reached for it—then frowned at the bent shaft in his fist.

He nodded at the arrow without comment, assuming it must have come close to snapping when she'd grabbed it at a gallop.

"Guess it won't be very lucky anymore," she said lightly, without a shade of remorse.

Still frowning, his gaze was drawn to hers. Although she smiled, an angry, contained fire danced behind her smoke-blue eyes. "I could give you some suggestions...of what you could do with it...next," she quietly stated.

Still nodding and frowning, he answered her. "Thank you, Captain. That won't be necessary."

For several heartbeats, her gaze didn't waver from his face, though his own was distracted by an evil curl of yellow in her hair, obscenely humping at her dark tresses. Caught in the dark mass of her hair, the angry wasp tried repeatedly to set his barb in her scalp, finding no solid ground for his penetration. As she started to turn, Dye stopped her with a word. "Martigay!"

Throwing a leg over his mount's neck, he slipped from the horse's back. His hand shot toward her head and she flinched but held her ground. Crushing the wasp in his fist, he realized that she'd thought he would strike her. Slowly, he unwound his fist and showed her the insect in his hand. Several seconds were lost as he watched her gaze go to his palm then flick to his face with the first real warmth he'd ever seen in her eyes.

She'd taken his action as an offering of peace, apparently touched by the fact that he hadn't wanted to see her harmed...despite his earlier, antagonizing behavior.

"You're stung," she murmured as she took his hand in both of hers, drawing it toward her breast.

"It's nothing," he argued, only now feeling the tiny bite of pain in the heel of his palm. And well worth it he decided in the next instant, glad he'd taken the sting he'd meant for her, as his fingers rested against the round warmth of her breast.

Very rapidly, a familiar ache grew in his loins and his flesh shivered as he was stabbed through with a shudder of physical need immediate and demanding. Her head dipped before he had a chance to react and the next thing he felt were her lips on his palm, a strange, deep warmth and then her teeth pulling the stinger he had thought too deeply set to be retrieved.

Just as he'd thought the arrow so deeply set.

Abruptly, the warmth was gone as her hands curled his knuckles closed and she spat on the ground, clearing the stinger from her mouth.

He was surprised to find his other hand curled around her upper arm, gently holding her—keeping her—before him. Beneath his fingers was the rough, puckered surface of the long, evil scar that tore a line down the back of her arm. Gently, he ran his fingertips along its length. As if in answer, she pulled away, shuddering.

"Is there a story that goes with that scar?" he asked her gently, before she could escape him.

Her eyes flashed with unexpected, uncharacteristic panic.

"I'm sorry," he murmured in concern. "Is it something you'd rather not talk about?"

"My Lord," the words seemed to strangle her, "it's something I'd rather not *think* about." Abruptly, she turned, taking her warmth with her as he watched her back, absently reaching behind him for his horse's reins. It took a few pawing swipes to locate them.

Mithra and Donar Together at Once! Did blue eyes ever get any prouder? Was there a more defiant chin anywhere in the world? Was there a more impudent nose? And what did she do to her hair? It was the richest, darkest shade of red he'd ever seen—bar none—all the way down to her shoulders. In waves.

In waves, he thought, and shook his head again. Thick glossy waves a man could knot around his fingers, and use to drag a woman's face—

Her legs, clad in tight doeskins.

Nay, he decided abruptly, he wouldn't think of her legs. His imagination had a tendency to keep wrapping them around his hips. As he resolved to abandon this line of thought, his mind halted, rested and languished on her impressively bold, round breasts and he groaned—audibly. Her nipples didn't show through the doeskin jerkin she wore. He regretted that. Regretted that with all his heart as well as with every single inch of his rigid, aching cock.

Raising his fist to his mouth, he stroked the heel of his palm with his bottom lip. His little ruse to put the proud sprite in her place hadn't turned out exactly as he'd anticipated. He'd put her in her place, all right—and now found her permanently placed at the forefront of his very distracted attention, when his intent had been the utter opposite.

Chapter Five

"Did you want me, sir?"

Dye looked up from his conversation with his scout. Martigay stood just inside his tent. "Aye," he said, without thinking, as he stared at her a few more unthinking seconds. "Aye." Determinedly, he lowered his eyes to the parchment on the table. "I have a message to go out to all of my lieutenants based on new scouting reports."

The army was still more than a day's ride from the outlying towns of Amdahl, but Saharat riders had been sighted in the south and the news of his army's approach would soon reach the enemy. An update would have to be sent to his lieutenants, each of whom were separated by about half a league's distance in order to assure grazing for the army's mounts. "It will be a minute. Take a seat, Martigay. Thank you, Brand."

Dismissed, the man seated before the king stood, saluted, and smiled at Martigay on his way across the tent.

Martigay slouched lazily in her chair. "What's with him?" she asked on the scout's departure.

Dye gave her five seconds of impatient silence. "If you mean my Scout Captain — Brand — he's a Raith."

The girl's jaw dropped. "No! A Raith? Really? Do all of them have blue hair?"

"As far as I know, they do. They're fairly rare this far north. You've never seen one before?"

She shook her head. "Is it true they can disappear? Become invisible?"

"Not disappear. Dematerialize."

"Dema..."

"Like a ghost. Without substance. But you can't tell when a Raith is dematerializing, because they don't look any different when they're doing it. You can't...see through them," he finished.

"Really!" She stared at the door thoughtfully. "He had nice eyes," she said slowly, and turned her own smoke-blue eyes on the king.

"I hadn't noticed," he grunted.

"That must make them impossible to hit in battle," she said, picking up their earlier thread of conversation.

Dye shook his head. "They can't keep it up indefinitely. Only as long as a few heartbeats. But," he stopped significantly, "that can be long enough to pass through the thick walls of a battlement."

Martigay appeared to think about this. "What happens to their clothing?" she asked with a grin. "Do they come out naked on the other side?"

Dye rolled his eyes. "They're able to take their clothing with them, as well as anything they're carrying. Some of them, in fact, are strong enough to take larger things with them, so long as they're touching them."

Martigay shrugged. "You mean like a trunk full of treasure? Another person?"

"Only the strongest Raith could take someone with him," he told her brusquely, scratching out the quick message on a short scroll of parchment. He slapped it into her hand. "Have each of my lieutenants read this. When you're done, report back to me." When she stood and turned, he watched her swagger out of the tent, his eyes locked on her shapely derriere.

Upon his exit a few moments later, Dye's eyes swept his environs briefly. His army's tents were randomly spaced, separated at wide intervals on the rolling meadow of short, pale grass. As he began to turn, he stopped instead, slapping his gloves in his hand. About fifteen paces distant, at the meadow's edge, Martigay stood head to head with the Raith. Brand's head dipped to meet hers as if they shared some intimate secret just before the scout grabbed her by the waist and threw her on her horse. Roughly, the man squeezed her upper thigh then reached for his own mount, threw himself into the saddle, and spurred away.

Dye heard her laugh and call out parting words as he turned on his heel and put the girl behind him. Several jarring steps later he realized he was grinding his teeth and made a mental effort to halt the action. As she passed him, mounted on her pony, she turned her body to salute the king with a closed fist.

Irritated and annoyed — at the girl, her salute, his scout, and at his own unexpected reaction to the sight of Brand's hand on her thigh — he sought her feelings and…came up empty!

Again, he set his mind to scan her feelings before she was out of range and again he felt nothing. With uneasy suspicion tugging at his senses, his eyes narrowed on her back as he watched the paint canter out of camp.

From his Westerman grandfather he'd inherited the ability to see in the dark. From his Slurian grandmother had come the capacity to sense others' emotions — so long as he was within thirty feet of the subject. Never in his life had he run across a man or woman he couldn't read. Of course, he hadn't tried to read *everyone* he came into contact with, but generally he was aware of a person's feelings without trying. It was odd that he hadn't noticed the absence before, but most of his encounters with the little soldier hadn't been one on one. More often than not, she was surrounded by the rest of his army. He'd not have noticed her absence of emotion in a crowd of people.

And when he *was* alone with her, she was…such a damned distraction. Now he walked slowly through the camp scanning for another anomaly, finding none. Apparently Captain Martigay was an enigma, he concluded. A very curious aberration.

It was late in the day before she returned from her task and sauntered into his tent, a plate of stew in one hand, a slab of fry bread in the other. Motioning her into a chair, Dye continued through several pieces of correspondence while she ate. At the end of each item, he scanned — tentatively — across the space that separated them, probing for any trace of emotion. Eventually giving up, he wondered if the woman was somehow able to sense and block his probe. A few surreptitious glances in her direction revealed nothing in her expression to indicate that was the case.

"You were gone longer than necessary," he said shortly.

Martigay nodded around a mouthful of hot bread. "Your lieutenants had a lot to say."

"How's that?"

"Sir?"

"What did my lieutenants have to say?"

She shook her head. "There were no messages for you, sir."

"That's not what I asked, soldier."

Martigay stopped chewing and stared at him for two instants. Swallowing the bread, she leaned back in her chair.

"Thank you, Martigay," she recited, "how's it going? How do you like being the king's messenger? Never mind, you'll get used to him. Really! I didn't know that! Well, I expect we'll all have to get used to him, then.

"Hey, Martigay. Thanks for the message. What kind of mood is he in today? Uh-huh. Uh-huh. Thanks for the warning. Right. Watch yourself, girl. The man has no sense of humor.

"Martigay! I wasn't expecting you! Do you have time to stop? I've some tea brewing. I won't keep you long. Okay, then, if you must. What did you decide about tomorrow night? Are we still on for—?"

"Thank you, Captain."

Martigay regarded the king with eyes full of life and laughter. "Were you born without a sense of humor or have you worked hard at it all your life?"

He ignored the impertinence of her remark. "Do *you* take nothing seriously?"

"Sex," she said.

"What?"

"I take sex seriously. What about you?"

"You want to know what I take seriously?"

Martigay rolled her eyes. "No. I think I've got that bit puzzled out, sir. What I'm wondering is—how you feel about sex." When there was no response, she continued. "Is there anything you pursue at your leisure, anything you do without purpose, without ambitious intent?"

His mouth was a flat line in his face.

"Not even sex?"

"Nay."

The girl shifted lazily in her chair. "Glad to hear it," she murmured to no one in particular. "You don't believe in meaningless sex, then." Eyes full of teasing challenge, she returned her gaze to his.

He stared at her a long, hard time. "I might be willing to make an exception," he finally said, "under the right circumstances."

Her lips parted in a devilish grin that was filled with pleased mischief.

And the king smiled.

His lips tilted up and the hard vertical lines on either side of his mouth curved as they gave way to the smile. The warmth of that rare smile moved Martigay to action. Shoving backward in her chair, Martigay rose as she stretched in a yawn, knowing her doeskin jerkin pulled tight across her chest as her breasts thrust forward.

"Well, I'm off to bathe," she announced loudly. "Think I'll just wander downstream a ways—probably about five hundred paces—and...bathe." Her left eyebrow made an arch of amusement just before she turned and swung her hips in a sauntering exit.

* * * * *

She was rubbing henweed into her hair as he climbed onto the rise of rock overhanging the pool. An early sunset slashed across the lowering clouds, splashing them deep rose and cyan. The late light spilled onto the water in a wash of rose madder and ultramarine as warm hues of rose and pink separated out to mingle with brooding, solemn purples, merging into bruised shades reminiscent of a woman's sex-roughened flesh—and a man's dark, intrusive need.

Crouching on the rock above her, Dye watched Martigay bend over in the shallow water, presenting her perfect bottom for his appraisal and appreciation. He held his breath at the sight of her rounded cheeks enclosing the deep, pink heart of her sex. When his cock shifted to uncoil inside his leggings, he reached down to rearrange his length.

Turning and straightening, she looked up as he did so. "You going to sit there watching all day?" she called up to him. "Or are you coming down here?"

"I've a country to run," he told her. "A war to win."

Crushing the stalks of henweed between her palms, she rubbed them into the pubic hair that curled on her mound. "Take a break, My Lord. Come down here and be a man for an hour, if you haven't forgotten how to."

Dye watched her without smiling. "I don't fuck my soldiers," he told her, his voice sharp and clear as it traveled across the open water.

She didn't seem put off. "Is that in the Handbook?" He raised one eyebrow in question. "The Commander's Handbook of Appropriate Comportment?"

"Aye," he growled, "It is. Scroll 10, Paragraph 3, underlined in red. The Leader of the Army shall not fuck his soldiers."

Martigay quirked a grin at him. "Sound policy, I would guess, for the most part."

"For the most part." The king nodded his agreement. "Since I'm not one for men and most of my army is male."

"There are exceptions," she reminded him. "As you pointed out."

"And the exceptional," he murmured quietly.

"What's that, My Lord?"

Clearing his throat, he immediately improvised. "There are exceptions," he agreed. "I've two units of slingers," he admitted. "And some women in the archers. I worked with women in Khal."

"And you never…"

He shook his head, squinting off into the distance.

"Never tempted?"

Not like this, he thought. He shook his head again.

"By anyone under your command?"

By anyone, he realized. By anyone in his entire life. Not that there hadn't been plenty of women, only that there'd never been one he couldn't walk away from. Again, he wished he could read her feelings. Find out what motive she had in tempting him. Was it only lust, or something more—or only something less?

Pure mischief.

Was it anything more than she felt for that sergeant who was always with her—Palleden? Was it anything more than she felt for Brand? His teeth clenched at the thought of the scout's hands around her waist, then high on her thigh. Too high.

Damn.

Gazing down on her, he longed to feel her skin beneath his hand, longed to feel her nipples tighten inside his palm. His hands ached to follow her curves. His fingers itched to sneak into her dark, female places and explore everything a woman kept hidden from a man. Briefly, he considered joining her—not long enough to compromise himself or his principles, just long enough to get his body up against hers—just long enough to absorb and savor the touch of her soft, damp curves pressed warmly against the hard length of his body.

He shook his head, knowing he'd never be able to stop there.

He wanted her more than he'd ever wanted anything. Wanted to bury himself between her legs, cram her cunt full of his cock and pound his way to some kind of peace by spilling inside of her. He gazed down at her naked chest, the ruddy light glinting on her wet curves and wanted to smother himself, face down, between the soft, full pillows of her breasts, to scrape his tongue over every centimeter of those considerable breasts and eat at her nipples while he covered her hand with his own and wrapped her fingers around his dick.

She would have to be the hottest little fuck ever.

"Last chance," she warned with a laugh, stretching her arms over her head provocatively.

From the rock above her, Dye watched as she turned her sexy pose into a dive that took her to the middle of the pool. Her bottom flashed at the water's surface an instant before disappearing from view.

I've a country to run, a war to win, and a princess to wed. And if I go down there, he told himself morosely, *I might not care about any of it anymore.*

With this thought, Dye straightened and turned, putting the pool and the woman at his back. Still, he lingered, allowing the liquid sounds of movement to tease his senses, his mind eagerly supplying pictures to go with the sounds as he snapped a thin branch from a nearby bush and stripped the tender bark away with his fingernails.

Inside the confines of his loose doeskins, his cock stretched and lengthened as lust surged thick through his bloodstream and pooled like a heavy weight in his groin. With a sharp groan of frustration, he threw the naked twig to the ground and stalked back toward camp.

* * * * *

Pronking little imp of a tease, he was still telling himself the next morning—long past the point at which he should have forgotten the whole incident at the pool. Brazen little flirt! Stumbling on a rock, Dye fought to regain his balance and continued toward the mess tent, tugging at the mass of tangled rope in his hands.

He'd fallen asleep with Martigay's naked image engraved in his consciousness and woken to find the same nude sprite bathing on the inside of his closed eyelids. Somehow it didn't help when he'd opened his eyes. She was still there, bending over the water, the late light of early evening spilling the colors of sex upon her skin, the water wet and slick, coating her ass like a man's shining ejaculate.

Like *his* shining ejaculate.

He imagined his hand on the wet curving flesh of her bottom, smoothing his cum to cover the silky surface of her skin.

If only she wasn't in his army. He'd lay her in a heartbeat, Bruthinia notwithstanding. Fuck her right out of his system so he could get on with his duties without any further…distraction. In his thirty-odd years, he'd walked away from more women than he could count—let alone remember. Yet, all of those experiences combined were not as hard as yesterday…walking away from that little upturned ass beckoning him down off his rock to wade crotch-deep into Martigay's waters.

* * * * *

From the corner of her eye, Martigay caught a flash of gold and red, indicating the king approached the open mess tent. Quickly, she threw her feet up on the table in a casual pose as she loosened the ties at her chest. At the same time, she pulled her lips through her teeth to fatten and redden them. Setting her lips in a provocative pout, she kept her eyes on him as he swept beneath the canvas sheltering the camp's kitchen.

Preoccupied by the long snarl of rope he carried, Dye was halfway into the tent before a glance at his surroundings got caught up on Martigay.

Hung up on Martigay.

And stuck there.

Martigay's smile was pure, gratified satisfaction as Dye walked right into a heavy wooden bench. She watched as he fought to keep his balance, his gaze still locked with hers.

The merry bell of her laughter made Dye's mouth draw into a tight, hard line. Slapping the rope against his thigh, he detoured in her direction to tower over her, his face cold and threatening. At his back, three men shuffled out of the tent, leaving the two of them alone but for the cook who was sergeant of the mess tent.

"Captain Martigay." Disconnecting his gaze, Dye's eyes plowed across the room, over his captain's head, as he set himself the task of looking anywhere but at that provocative face. "I'm pleased you find me—and my knees—such a ready source of amusement. Perhaps you could do me a favor in return." The tangle of rope landed on the table just south of her feet. "I've a few knots in my coil."

Martigay eyed the mess on the table then gave him her attention. "I doubt the rope is in knots, sir...unless My Lord put them there purposefully." Her feet slid to the floor as her fingers crept across the table and she held his eyes with hers. "Did you?"

"Of course not," he gritted at her.

With her foot, she pushed a chair out for him on the opposite side of the table.

Grinding his jaw, he considered the chair.

"In that case, the rope won't be knotted. It's only tangled. And normally, when things tangle, they get tangled in pairs."

Motioning to the army cook, Dye snorted as he dropped into the chair, curious to see how far she would take this bit of nonsense. "And what's that supposed to mean? I suppose the next thing you'll tell me is that it takes two to tangle."

Her fingers tugged at the cord.

"Well?" he prompted her.

"Yes, sir. You're not far off in that assessment. See here, where two lengths of cord lie together. The key to unraveling a knotted rope is to follow the pair to where they join, looped together at the head. Then," she said softly, "find where the loop is constricted and tease the loop free." She demonstrated.

Quietly, without comment, he watched her work the rope through several tight constrictions. "What now, soldier?" he asked her, as he saw a cord now split the loop she'd been working with. "You've reached the end of your rope," he pointed out, reaching for the mug of steaming chicory when the cook placed it on the table.

She shook her head slowly, eyes still on his, as her fingers worked the cord deftly. "Now you look for the next loop."

Dye tilted his head. "I don't see another."

"It's there, nonetheless. It's only a matter of finding it. Here we are," she said gently, and he watched her stroke her fingers through the thick cords just before her hands wrapped and slid, suggestively, along a whole handful of thick rope. All at once, she lifted the heavy skein, gave it a shake and held the orderly length out toward him. Returning his clay mug to the table, he reached to take the rope from her. Her fingers touched his as he did so, causing his eyes to lock on hers.

She gave him a long, warm, sultry look. "Next time you have a knot in your coil, come to me first. I'll be happy to straighten you out."

His voice was a quiet warning. "Don't tangle with me, Martigay."

"It takes two to tangle," she reminded him lazily as she pushed back in her chair. "Like anything else, sir, the key to unknotting life's obstacles is a little confidence and a great deal of patience."

Together they stood, the king with the rope on his shoulder and the mug of hot brew clamped in a fist held tightly against his chest—the mug and the fist a boundary marker staked between him and the girl. But Martigay pushed in close to him—the bold little hussy—her full breasts bracketing his mug to warm his clenching fist.

"Fortunately, My Lord, I have both."

Her face was tilted upward, her lips mere inches from his as he vaguely noted the cook departing the mess tent on some errand. His eyes were on her lush, parted lips as his white-knuckled fingers tightened around the handle in his fist and a warning shiver of tension traveled across the surface of the hot chicory. As his doubled fist expanded and filled the tight space inside the handle, there was a sharp retort of sound at the same time the handle separated from the cup and the clay mug exploded in his hand.

She jumped away from the spill of hot liquid that burst in his hand and spattered down the front of his body. Crushing the remnant of mug still in his fist, Dye stared down at his stained doeskins then at Martigay, untouched by a single dark drop. Angrily flinging the broken clay to the ground, his left hand shot out to manacle her right wrist, twisting her arm behind her before she could finish the breath she'd started. The next thing she knew, her cheek was pressed against the wooden table top as he doubled her body over the table and kicked her legs apart, placing his feet just inside hers.

With his crotch jammed tight against her firm little bottom, he leaned into her as she finally finished that breath she'd started earlier with an audible gasp.

"Don't push me, girl," he told her in a quiet voice of menace. "Or you'll find yourself ass-up over a table with my cock buried between your cheeks while I pump myself off inside you."

With an upward jerk of his hips, he pushed the thick mound of his groin into her crease. "You might think it a fine ambition to make love to a king, but I'll remind you — it's not so long since I was a very *common* soldier with only a very *rough* taste in women. I'm not picky about where and when and how. And I don't care who's watching when I'm fucking a woman up against a wall in some back alley or over a table in a crowded tavern. I'm warning you, Captain Martigay — you dick with me and you won't walk for a week."

With this exaggerated threat and a separating thrust, he pushed himself away from her as she whipped around to face him. Her hair tumbled around her face and her eyes glinted with a smoky fire as two bright points of rose burned high on her cheekbones.

"Don't make me break my own rule, soldier. Stay away from me or you *will* get fucked," he told her in soft, cutting words. "And it *won't* be nice. Have I made myself clear, Captain?"

"Just one thing, Commander," she stuttered back at him, obviously shaken, but tossing her proud head to move her dark hair out of her eyes. She took a deep breath and plunged on. "Is that a threat, sir? Or a promise?"

Chapter Six

Situated now for several days within a few hours ride of the walled city, Dye had moved his army and set up camp at a village on the outskirts of Amdahl. The many tents of his soldiers surrounded and almost engulfed the small hamlet, and though the inhabitants were awed by the sudden influx of men from the north, they adjusted rapidly to the influx of wealth and supplies that accompanied it, happily offering services in return. Only the young men of the village glowered when the local girls flirted with the soldiers of his army. Yet more than one of the same young men was caught with his eyes following the confident stride of a group of slingers making their way along the beaten track that traveled through town.

Dye found himself avoiding Martigay whenever possible, sending the messages she was to carry through the hands of his attendants, keeping to the small inn that he'd made his headquarters, striding through his army's camp with his eyes straight ahead.

Anything to stay away from her.

Then, all at once looking for her, calling for her on a pretense when there was no real need for her services. Wandering through camp without purpose, hoping to catch a glimpse of her.

In the middle of the night, he'd find himself standing outside the inn, sleepless, his eyes drawn to her shelter — always able to identify her tent, regardless of its location because of the light she kept all night, painting the canvas walls of her shelter a pale yellow.

Watching from a distance one night, he saw her shadow moving on the yellow canvas and he held his breath, hoping for a glimpse of her undressing as she readied herself for bed. But the outline of her body melted into the ground and he watched intently as she struggled out of her clothes while lying on the mat. Staring at the blank canvas, he hated her for this stingy, prim withholding. Glancing around the camp, he realized that other men might be watching, as well, and immediately loved her for the same act of modesty. Then—at the thought of other men—he stood there for some time, watching long enough to assure himself she was alone.

* * * * *

Finding himself staring at the ceiling one evening, Dye shook himself.

Is that a threat, sir? Or a promise?

Her defiant voice rang in his head as he smiled. For the first time in ages, he felt alone, wishing a friend was there to share the story with. Shuffling through the correspondence on his table, he picked up the missive that had arrived earlier in the day—sent by his sister from Tharran. Petra and her husband, Davik, the King of Khal along with Davik's brother, Warrik, were on their way south with four thousand Khallic volunteers. He expected their arrival two days hence. Dye stared at the curling parchment for several moments then tossed it back on the pile, reaching for his cloak as he headed toward the nearest tavern. Warrik would want to meet her, he decided, impatiently waving off his guard when they tried to follow him.

Dye stepped inside the crowded tavern, backing toward the wall as his pupils opened in the dim, smoke-filled room. The large inn was packed with tight knots of people who alternately laughed, sang, fought, argued or gamed. Drawing his hood down to cover his hair and shadow his features, he pushed around the crowd at the perimeter of the room.

He found her when he heard his name.

"Dye? The King? Oh, he's a clever enough commander," she was saying. "Competent leader. Can't fault him there. But man, the guy needs to develop a personality." She snorted. "Any sort of personality. Even a bad one." She laughed. "Even a closet personality. The poor guy's so busy being King and Commander, so busy being a cold bastard bent on discipline—"

Someone cut her off. "Can't lead an army and be everyone's friend, Martigay."

She swigged at her ale and wiped her mouth. "The king isn't *anyone's* friend. I pity his betrothed, Bruthinia. The guy has no sense of humor, talks about nothing outside of his work and is completely lacking feelings—or anything else that might be mistaken for warmth or passion."

As she said this, Martigay elbowed the man who crowded her back and pushed herself forward to put some distance between herself and the man behind her. She made a face. "Who wants a guy like that in her bed?" she demanded as the large man behind her loomed over her. With an elbow, she nudged him back.

"I wouldn't mind giving him a try," a tall, blonde archer spoke up cheerfully. "Just once. Maybe twice," she laughed. "You would too, Martigay! Don't deny it!"

Martigay beat the suggestion off with an offended look.

"Yes, you would!"

Martigay just grinned.

Again, she was crowded from behind. Impatiently she crouched and threw her elbow back hard to clear the space behind her.

Dye's hood flew back just before he doubled slightly. Stunned silence radiated outward from the king in an ever-widening ring of stillness. The tavern went dead quiet as the inn's clientele realized that the king was in their midst...and exactly where Martigay had elbowed him.

Annoyed, Martigay turned to face the man at her back and locked eyes with the king, his blue eyes bright with pain.

"My Lord," she gasped.

He raised a hand to stop her. "Please, Captain Martigay," he choked out, still bending slightly at the waist. "I'm fine. Fortunately for me, I'm a cold bastard without feelings. Otherwise, the unfortunate placement of your elbow might have caused me some discomfort. I appreciate your commendation of my leadership capabilities," he added, drawing his cloak around himself and moving toward the tavern's door. When he reached it, he turned back. In all this time, he hadn't smiled.

"And I'll work on my sense of humor. Report to me early tomorrow. I'll have some new orders for you that I, at least, will find amusing."

Chapter Seven

Martigay reported to the king's office early the next dawning. "My cook is ill," he told her without looking at her, "you can take his place this evening."

What! Martigay clamped down on her teeth to keep back the protest that leapt to her tongue. "Sir. Are you displeased with me?"

"I'm displeased with your attitude, soldier. As well as your salute."

"My salute? I…I'm sorry, sir. The fist…it's an old habit. I'll work on it."

"You can work on it in my kitchen."

She stood before him like a piece of stone. "Is this because of what happened last night, in the tavern?"

Finally, he looked up at her. "You're dismissed, Captain Martigay."

"Captains…" she said, almost choking on the words, "don't work in the kitchen…sir."

"This one does."

"Sir —"

Dye exploded out of his seat, almost tipping it behind him. "Captain Martigay, I have twelve thousand soldiers under my command and *you* are the *only* one who can't follow orders! You're right!" he said in a sudden fire of frustration. "Captains don't work in the kitchen. Pawyns, however, do."

Still she stood there.

"You're *dismissed*, Pawyn Martigay. You can leave your ribbon on the table."

Slowly, she nodded her head. "I'm sorry, sir, if I'm a bit slow. I was just thinking, sir. About your betrothed, Bruthinia."

"What about Bruthinia?" he snapped.

"I was thinking, sir, that if you were my husband, I'd slit my wrists."

"And if you were my wife," he snarled back at her, "I'd sharpen your knife for you—every morning, *first thing!*"

Her eyes gleamed that strange metallic warning before she turned abruptly and headed through the arch toward his kitchen.

Jaw clamped with the bone-crushing force of a bear trap, Dye turned to drag both hands through his hair, tight against his skull.

Cold bastard—completely lacking anything that might be mistaken for passion!

Dye swallowed the roar of frustration that tried to surface. *If she only knew!* If she only knew the depth of savage emotion she evoked in him. Dye shook his head as he turned back to stare toward the kitchen.

He took a deep, steadying breath.

She was wrong, of course. She was wrong. And he wasn't going to lie to himself about it. This had nothing to do with what had happened in the tavern the previous night. Though he had expected her to think so, the incident in the tavern was an excuse at best.

And not an excuse to punish her, either.

Mithra, no.

But it was an excuse, all right. An excuse to have her close by for most of a day.

He still wanted Warrik to meet her, and he still had an invitation to issue.

* * * * *

There was a clatter of metal and pottery as Martigay pushed through the cupboard, humming as she searched through the inn's tableware. Finally finding what she wanted, she headed back to the fire with a large brass goblet in one hand and a jar of wine in the other.

She smiled to herself, well aware that the king was following her actions from the adjoining room. Although he scratched through his correspondence with his head lowered, the blaze of his blue gaze lifted to settle on her frequently. Each time it did, his expression was coldly appraising, as though he merely sought to assure himself that she was still there and still working.

But Martigay didn't really care why he watched her. Andarta! The man was the most delicious thing she'd ever set eyes on. He made her burn. He made her damp from the knees on up! Damned if she wasn't going to have him, one way or another. Martigay nodded to herself. She was going to get down and dirty with the king if it was the last thing she did—and she wasn't beyond a dirty trick or two to get him exactly where she wanted him.

Between her legs.

Placing the jar and goblet on a table, she surveyed her hands thoughtfully as she considered the idea of dirty tricks. Quickly, she turned and crossed the kitchen to step outside. Grabbing up a bucket of water, she dashed it on the ground and stooped to rub her hands into the muddy puddle she'd created. Returning to the kitchen, she regarded her dirty fingernails with satisfaction as she picked up the wine and goblet again.

Dye started when she slammed the goblet down under his nose and slopped wine into it. It was the biggest damn goblet he'd ever seen in his life. With his forearm, he swept his correspondence aside before the wine could stain his work.

"That's enough," he tried to tell her, but she continued to splash out the wine, ignoring him. "What are you doing, soldier? I said that's enough."

Martigay hummed as she poured. "What am I doing? If you must know, sir, I'm going to get you drunk."

"And why would you do that?"

"I have my reasons, sir."

Dye opened his mouth then froze when he noticed her hands. "Didn't you wash your hands?" he choked out.

"Sir?"

"Your hands! Did you not wash them before you prepared the meal?"

Martigay raised her hands slowly to her face, frowning at her filthy paws just before she shrugged. "I told you I wasn't a cook," she said carelessly. With a flippant twist of her hips, she turned back into the small kitchen. "Your meal will be out in an instant, sir."

Dye watched her hips swing toward the kitchen. Her doeskin leggings stretched tight across her shapely bottom and her grimy hands were all but forgotten as her tiny waist and round derriere seemed somehow far more important to him at that particular moment in time. As she'd promised, she was back in an instant, carrying a pottery plate in one dirty mitt.

"What is it?" Dye stared at the plate she'd dropped in front of him. It appeared to be a stew of some sort though he couldn't remember ever eating anything quite that shade of yellow before.

"I'm not sure, sir. I don't think it tastes as bad as it smells."

"Well, I hope it tastes better than it looks." He slanted a suspicious glance in her direction. "Perhaps you should taste it for me."

"Sir!" The girl regarded him with alarm.

"Better still," he growled, "why don't you join me, Martigay?" He pushed the plate toward her as she backed away. "What did you do," he asked her tightly, "poison my food?"

Her chin came up. "You'd deserve it, if I had."

"Well, as long as it's not poisoned, you can join me. No reason I should suffer alone," he muttered, pulling the plate back toward him and stirring his spoon into the unappetizing mess.

"I'd rather not, sir. I have…other duties."

"Sit down," he growled, and she lowered herself, reluctantly, onto the stool beside him. Digging his spoon into the yellow muck, Dye pointed the wooden utensil at her mouth. "Open up," he ordered, dragging her stool closer to his chair.

She opened her mouth a fraction and he slipped the spoon between her lips. Making a face, she swallowed the stuff down.

Eyes keenly lit, he watched her face. "How is it?"

"Try it yourself."

"If you're still alive in five minutes, I will." Again, he dug some of the stew from the plate and forced it between her lips. This time she swallowed more willingly and, with this encouragement, Dye carefully licked the back of the spoon. His eyebrows shot upward. "It's good!"

"It ought to be," she muttered. He looked at her questioningly. "I found your cook's bottle of saffron."

"How much did you use?"

"A year's supply would be my guess," she muttered.

"What?"

"The whole bottle, sir."

"A whole bottle! Saffron costs…a fortune, Martigay."

"Better eat it, then. I wouldn't want to be responsible for wasting the king's money."

As Dye cleared his plate, Martigay was fidgeting in her seat. When he offered her the last spoonful, she shook her head, but his threatening glare convinced her to open her mouth. Her eyes closed as her luscious lips went around the spoon. Slowly, she opened sultry eyes to his and his cock stretched inside his leggings.

All at once, a hard cramp of immediate need forcefully below the belt as his cock thickened with an that was nothing short of painful. Drawing in a harsh gas hand clutched the nearest available surface and tightened on...Martigay's knee. Staring into her eyes, he found them filled with the same smoldering lust that possessed him.

"*What*—" he choked out, "what did you *do*, Martigay?" Her eyes lowered slowly to the hand clamped on her knee and she moaned. "What *else* went into the stew, besides saffron?" His eyes widened. "Cadaridaes," he whispered. "You put cadaridaes in the stew? You put an *eroticant* in the stew?" he shouted. "How much?"

"How much does two silver buy?"

"*I'll kill you*," he hissed and made a grab for her. Getting to her feet in a great hurry, Martigay pushed away from him, stumbling backward. "Oh no you don't," he gasped, catching her before she could fall. "If I'm going to suffer, you'll suffer with me, girl."

His blunt fingers bit into her arms and her eyes grew wide as she gazed up at him...without a trace of alarm. Instead her eyes were filled with warm anticipation, shaded with sultry undertones. Her voice was breathy when she said, "If you say so, sir. Only, I doubt I'll suffer much."

In one sharp instant, Dye registered understanding and he almost screamed in frustration. "You fed me cadaridaes so you could...*take advantage* of me?"

She nodded. "And don't forget the wine, sir. There was all that wine as well." Slowly, her lips gravitated toward his.

Dye jerked his face away from her. "Well," he hissed, "you're not getting any, Martigay. You're never getting any! You little *imp* of a whore! How could you—" He halted, staring at her luscious wet lips shining inches from his own, and he groaned. "Do you want to know what you're not getting? Do you, Martigay? Shall I show you?"

As he dragged her across the room, she stumbled to her knees and he jerked her back to her feet, turning her to face the wall and pinning her there with his body. He shuddered as his body absorbed the touch of the woman curving beneath him, and squeezed into her more tightly. The anxious length of steel that was his erection found its way between the cheeks of her bottom and he moved against her, mindless with need, his cock almost bursting with agonizing pressure, his testes as tight and solid as two iron balls. A little friction on the taut, stretched skin of his shaft and he began to come in a series of blindingly hot, scalding surges. Opening his mouth, he buried it in the tender stretch of her neck as he strangled the roar of pure, perfect agony that exploded up the column of his throat.

Martigay felt Dye's damp lips on her neck, his teeth just short of breaking her skin as his groin pounded her lower body into the wall. The rhythmic contact of her mons with the wall's smooth wood drove her inflamed pussy to within a fraction of orgasm. When Dye stopped moving, frozen in his own arrival, she rubbed her rise against the wall as she tried to take herself that last fraction down the road to orgasm. Desperately close to climax, she moaned against the wall.

At that wanton sound, Dye's semi-rigid cock surged back to aching attention and renewed need. Turning her in a flash of unthinking passion, he pinned her wrists beside her face and smashed his body against hers. He could smell the lust-drug on her breath as the thick ridge of his cock dragged over her rise, digging into her belly as she rose to her toes, trying to align her cleft with his dick.

Slowly, desperately, Martigay inched her foot up his calf, past his knee, trying to open her legs enough to catch some of him along her slot. Then his hard hand was on her bottom, lifting her, spreading her as his lower body hammered her into the wall at her back. She grunted and gasped as his erection made several scraping passes over her sensitive labia, knowing she was about two scrapes away from orgasm, struggling in his grasp, wanting to reach down with her hands and spread her labia to get the last piece of him she'd need to achieve orgasm.

He stopped suddenly, gasping roughly for breath. "You're not *getting* it, Martigay. You're not getting *any*, damn you. Don't even try." The girl whimpered as she tried to rock her body on his. "Do you want to *feel* what you're not getting? Do you want to see it? Taste it?"

"Dye," she moaned.

His name in her mouth, an uttered plea for help wrapped in the ragged whimper of a woman's need, drove him toward madness. Inching his body away from hers, he pulled his laces to free his angry cock. The hot, damp curve of flesh forced its way out of his leggings, the wide, plum-shaped head dark as a storm. Taking one of her hands, Dye wrapped it around the curving bow of his cock, groaning at the welcome contact of her cool palm on the burning flesh of his aching shaft.

Hooking a nearby stool with his foot, he dragged it to the wall and pushed her down to sit on it. Immediately, he straddled her legs, putting his flushed cock inches from her face.

"Here's a taste of it," he told her harshly. "A taste of what you'll never have." With his hand still wrapping hers around his dick, he nudged his cock head against her lips. A thick, pearly drop of his issue seeped from his slit and he ran the crown around the lush line of her lips, painting her pouting mouth slick with his glistening pre-cum.

This action was a mistake, he realized almost immediately, as his next impulse was to get his lips against hers. To taste his silver on her mouth, run his tongue around those glistening lips and then force it down her throat.

Before he had a chance to act on this impulse, the tip of her tongue flicked out to lick her upper lip. Her eyes closed an instant as she took his release into her mouth and her cheeks hollowed as she appeared to savor his taste. When she opened her eyes, her gaze focused on his cock with avaricious interest, and he groaned—knowing damn well what her next act would be. Swiftly unwinding her hand from around his shaft, he pulled out of her tight grip and backed away before she could get his cock into her mouth. Her eyes were lit with a desperate, hot fire as he backed away from her, her gaze fixed on his hand as his fist moved slowly at the base of his cock, two fingers resting low on his testes.

"Dye." The word was a low, breathy cry for help. Her hands were at her breasts, fumbling with the ties and he watched, mesmerized, as the jerkin opened in fits and bursts and she shrugged it off her shoulders. Stroking his dick out long and hard, he stared at her beautiful breasts straining beneath the thin fabric of her cotton chemise. He watched as she loosened the ties of her chemise, leaving the undergarment to hang open. The resulting view was a provoking one. The luscious inner curves of her breasts were boldly exposed in the narrow opening while her blushing areolas put in a shy appearance at the edges of the thin fabric.

Dye tilted his head, an unconscious attempt to see the rest of the way into her chemise, at the same time she was reaching for the ties on her leggings. Her hungry eyes were locked on his cock as she fought to get out of her doeskins.

"You're not *getting* it," he warned her as he pulled on the length of rigid, veined flesh in his fist.

As she lifted her bottom, struggling to get her leggings and shorts out of the way, he took a step toward her, spread his legs to straddle her again and bent his knees to put his cock between her breasts. His hard belly pushed her head into the wall as he rubbed his cock into the valley between her breasts a few times before he surged and spilled onto the naked skin of her chest.

Panting against her, he stood with his forehead against the wall.

"You're not getting it, Martigay," he moaned against the wall, feeling spent, hoping he was spent, knowing he wasn't when her lips brushed the taut skin stretching across his stomach. In a violent fit of frustration, he gathered himself enough to get his legs between hers and tried to spread them.

Her leggings still pinned her feet and he dropped to h̸
he dragged them away, bringing him face to face with̸
line of her pussy.

He halted as his eyes slowly traveled up her beautifully nude body. Carefully, he reached out one hand to draw the veil of her chemise aside and expose her dainty peach nipples. His eyes lingered there for several moments — on her nipples — before returning his gaze to the dark hair between her legs. Her warm, inviting thatch was deep red, violet red, almost purple.

Carefully, he pulled her legs open and watched the full, pouting lips of her vagina part. He glanced up at her face to find her head tilted back against the wall, her eyes closed as she sobbed shallowly. Inching her legs wider, he watched the line of her sex unfold — rutted, pink and glistening — moist with her female essence. Pulling her body forward to the stool's edge, he caught a glimpse of her opening and the wet rivulet that seeped from her vulva to dampen the stool's seat.

"Dye," she moaned, and he watched the hard tips of her breasts as her back arched and her nipples thrust upward, her body desperate for some kind of release. His dick was rock-hard again as he dragged her hands down to her pussy, and used her fingers to massage the top of her cleft. As she whimpered and gasped beneath her own hand, he massaged her until her slit was streaming. Abruptly, he stopped.

"Open your eyes," he demanded harshly. "I want you to *see* what you're not getting. Open your legs. All the way, Martigay." Dissatisfied with her idea of "all the way", he spread her legs with his elbows.

With his hand casing his shaft, he pumped himself as he rose to align his cock with her pussy. "Pay attention, Martigay, because *this* is what you're not getting. Open your eyes," he commanded roughly.

Her eyes opened in time to see his hot shot of release jump from his dick in a silver stream. As it hit her clitoris in a hot kiss, she exploded into orgasm, rocketing into a long, searing arrival with a cry that was almost painful.

Her body was like an explosion. Ruthlessly, Dye contained her as she jerked violently between his body and the wall, the length of her arrival far exceeding his own explosive release. Finally, she drew in a long sobbing breath and shivered. Dye's forehead hit the wall and for several moments they leaned against it together, panting, damp with perspiration, wet with sex shared and consummated.

By the time he caught his breath, he found himself on his knees between her legs, his arms wrapped tightly around her waist, his face buried between her breasts as her lips stirred in his hair. He *knew* he was in trouble. Knew he wanted *more* of her, knew he wouldn't be satisfied until he *got* more of her.

Feared he'd not be satisfied until he got *all* of her.

Thankful that the eroticant had apparently worn off, Dye heaved out a shuddering sigh of exhaustion. He remained kneeling while he pulled his ties to cover his damp, sticky cock, and watched Martigay move her legs together as she reached for her leggings and searched the floor. With a start of realization, he reached backward to grasp her jerkin, shaking it out while she pulled her doeskins up her legs. When he held it out to her, she slipped an arm through one hole as he brought the rest of it around her back.

It felt good, he realized—felt good wrapping her clothes around her. He wanted to wrap his arms around her and keep her there, wanted to wrap up that warmth and keep it for himself, alone—for the rest of…Mithra. What was he thinking?

Her chemise was still evocatively parted and her breasts hung, lush and full in the narrow opening, teasing his male senses with pitiless provocation. On his knees before her, he watched with a pang of regret as her cleavage disappeared beneath the strings she tightened across her chest.

Rising to his feet, he couldn't resist pursuing some sort of connection. He pulled her up with him and kept her hand. Awkwardly, he rasped her fingers in his as he struggled for something to say. "Did you…plan anything for dessert?" he asked finally, a little lamely.

She nodded down at her ties then looked up at him. Her face held a sad little smile. "I almost got it, too." When she withdrew her small hand from his, he relinquished his claim, but only with reluctance.

Brushing past him, she wobbled across the room and through the kitchen's arch.

"Martigay," he called out to her. She stopped in mid-wobble, turning back to him, but Dye didn't look at her. "You'll join me tomorrow evening at lastmeal."

"Dye... Sir?"

Looping a knot into his ties, he crossed the room to the table and picked up a piece of parchment. "I'm expecting guests from Khal. The new king and his wife. Davik of Khal is bringing four thousand Khallic volunteers to join our forces before we continue south."

"What!" Stunned, she bit the word back. "You're...going to have a *pawyn* sitting at your table along with your lieutenants and half the royalty of Khal?"

Producing a blue ribbon, he threw it on the table.

Martigay stared down at the bit of blue. Her voice started out an icy whisper, rising as she continued angrily. "You're going to *promote* me so I can have *lastmeal* with you! You're going to promote me so I can join your lieutenants and *eat* with you!"

Seeing the storm in her eyes, Dye moved to put the table between himself and the furious girl.

"I worked *months* for my promotion to sergeant. I saved a wagonload of your army's supplies for my next promotion to captain." As he dropped into his chair, she slammed her palms on the table and leaned over him. "Keep your damn ribbon and your *effing* promotion, man. Buy yourself a girl somewhere else."

She turned.

"Martigay!" He stood suddenly. "Pawyn or captain," his voice scraped, "you'll join me for lastmeal tomorrow." Martigay stood her ground. "My sister is wed to Davik of Khal. My lieutenants won't be joining me at the table. Only my sister and her husband. His brother, Warrik, will be there—my friends. I could use a woman at the table, company for Petra."

Slowly, Martigay turned back to face him. She looked angry at first, then haughty, then almost laughed. "As your date?"

There was an instant of silence wherein his jaw hardened. "If you'd like to think so."

"So you're asking me? It's not an order?" She watched a tic jump in his jaw. "I accept," she said quickly.

Dye nodded curtly. "You'll want to wear something...appropriate," he told her without looking at her worn doeskins. Stepping toward a trunk, he caught the lid with the toe of his boot and kicked it open. "I think you might find something to wear in here," he said, again without looking at her. "You'd look good in red," he told her as though it were an order.

"And put the ribbon back in your hair," he said more softly. She bit back her response as she watched him turn away from her, his arms crossed tightly across his chest. "I...was wrong in taking it from you."

Without excusing himself, he strode through the inn's door, leaving Martigay alone to rummage through the trunk. Frowning critically, she considered the heavy scarlet gown the king had...suggested. Cut out of thick velvet, with long sleeves and a high neckline that bordered on prim, she didn't think it was going to do the trick. She was having a hard enough time getting the king on the mat, without covering herself up in a wallowing great tent.

Martigay sighed. Generally, men weren't so reluctant to bed her. And normally it didn't require vast quantities of cadaridaes to get a man's cock out of his leggings.

Not that there'd been so many men.

But she did enjoy sex and took her woman's herbs every morning to prevent pregnancy—so she couldn't see any reason to deny herself the pleasure of a man's body. Martigay snorted. That didn't explain why she was holding out for the stubborn redhead. He was a challenge, she decided. That's why she hadn't...bothered with anyone else since she'd laid eyes on him.

He was a challenge, all right, she thought, considering the length of red velvet again.

Martigay shrugged. She liked a challenge.

From all indications, he'd be worth the effort. She nodded to herself, resurrecting the vision of Dye's thickly bowed flesh gripped in his fist as he pumped himself to splash between her legs. With the length of heavy velvet in one hand, she wandered toward the chair he'd occupied earlier. Her hand lingered to trail along the chair's wide back as she moved behind it. Coming around in front of Dye's chair, she lowered herself to sit, snuggling her bottom into the seat as she let her head fall back to rest her neck on the chair's broad back. After lifting a knee to drape over one of the chair's arms, she was ready to fully explore her feelings for the king.

The stubborn man fought his male instincts with such iron resolve and steel determination!

And he was *all* male!

He'd make someone a good husband, she decided with a nod to herself. Closing her eyes, she smoothed the lush fabric across her cheek and over her mouth, a deliberate effort to re-experience the light, velvet touch of Dye's cock head dragging over her lips, his male flesh a captivating combination of tender vulnerability and uncompromising steel.

As hard as lightning's blue edge, and as soft as a candle's warm glow, she mused.

Dipping her tongue into the corner of her mouth, Martigay lapped at his lingering taste, all rough and male and overpoweringly...Dye.

A rattle at the door opened her eyes. Dye stood just inside, staring transfixed as she sprawled in his chair, her legs spread in what must surely appear an open invitation. His lightning blue eyes burned beneath the warm glowing fire of his hair. Slowly, she smiled at him in an attempt underline the invitation.

Folding his arms across his chest, Dye leaned against the wall just inside the door as he continued his intent observation from the other side of the room.

Finally pulling her legs together, Martigay got to her feet. Andarta, the man was stubborn!

She could be stubborn, too, she decided, tossing the red dress aside.

Chapter Eight

Dye stared at the green dress hugging Martigay's glorious curves, the décolletage slashing almost to her waist, showing a good deal more of her cleavage than he wanted Warrik to see. "Perhaps I'm a fool," he said in a voice rimmed with ice, "but I thought you were told to wear red."

"You're right, sir—you're a fool."

This argument was interrupted in the next instant when a giant blond burst through the inn's doors. He took one look at Martigay and halted.

"Where'd you find this?" he exclaimed. "And tell me where I can get one."

"Where's your sword, Warrik?" Dye asked and Martigay wondered at the taunting edge that accompanied the question.

The big blond frowned at Dye. "I left the old battleaxe at home," he said, grasping Dye's forearm.

"And where'd you leave my sister?"

"Petra and Davik are right behind me...I think." Warrik shrugged. "You know how it is. A woman gets dressed up in something nice and she looks so good that...twenty minutes later she's getting dressed again." Grasping Martigay's arm, he pulled her close and kissed her with a great deal of energy.

"Don't let his enthusiasm fool you," Dye said when Warrik finally let her go. "The man's in love with his sword."

"Sir?"

The king made a face. "Call me Dye, Martigay, at least for this evening."

"Sir?"

"That's an order, Martigay." He pulled a chair out for her and she slid into it but was standing moments later for the King of Khal and his wife—Dye's sister—Petra.

Martigay felt like a shrimp.

They were all so tall, beginning with Warrik, who must have gone six foot seven, followed by Dye, a mere six-three, then the King of Khal, a few inches taller than his wife at perhaps six-two.

Both brothers were blond with blue eyes, though Warrik's hair trended more to gold than his younger brother's straw-colored mane, and Davik's eyes were more aqua than his older brother's cornflower blue.

The biggest surprise was Dye's sister who looked nothing whatsoever like her brother. Petra's skin was warm caramel as opposed to Dye's tawny tan, her eyes so dark a blue that they were almost as black as her long cascade of hair. The frayed ends of her hair tapered to tips of white, a telltale indication of Westerman blood.

With that thought, Martigay's gaze swung immediately to lock on Dye's. Her eyes narrowed as she observed the tiny black pinpoints that were centered in the volcanic blue of his irises. Westerman eyes! No doubt the king's night vision was as good as hers on a bright, cloudless day.

"This is Warrik's second time around," Dye was telling her.

"Sir—Dye?"

"Warrik was killed in the Civil War."

Warrik laughed. "You ought to know."

Dye nodded. "Warrik fought for the south. But, upon his death, Andarta resurrected him—"

"Andarta! The *goddess* Andarta?"

"So he could save her sisters," Dye finished.

Martigay looked impressed as she regarded the giant blond with new appreciation—appreciation that rubbed Dye the wrong way.

"Only with Dye's help," Warrik demurred gruffly and Dye felt a rush of gratitude toward him when Martigay's gaze swung back to his own face.

"It's a long story," Dye told her. "There's a full account written down somewhere. A pair of old harpies working out of a cave put it to paper. I'll try to find you a copy if you like."

"I'd like that."

Dye returned his attention to his friend. "What are you doing now, Warrik?"

Warrik rolled his huge shoulders in a shrug. "I've come down in the world," he admitted with a grin. "The man who was once the Heir to Khal is now leading a unit of Khallic Ir...regulars."

"Irreg—Northmen?"

Warrik nodded.

"*My* Northmen?"

Again, Warrik nodded. "Most like, you know some of the troops. Come by in the dawning and say hello."

At that point, the king's cook appeared at the door, directing a half dozen men with platters of food. Martigay smiled at the cook. "Feeling better, Sergeant Coopman?"

"Captain?" The king's cook took a second to check Martigay's hair and assure himself of her current rank. "Captain Martigay?"

Martigay's eyes flickered uncertainly from the cook to Dye and back again. "I thought you were ill yesterday."

"No, Captain. I was given the evening off."

Slowly, Martigay's eyes moved to connect with Dye's.

He returned her accusatory gaze without apology. "Sergeant Coopman," he said, "would you inform the captain of your new orders—your new orders concerning her."

The cook straightened and saluted his commander. "Sir. Henceforth, Captain Martigay is not permitted within ten paces of the kitchen. I am to use any and all means to secure the kitchen from Captain Martigay, including but not limited to the use of large, flat objects." Perfunctorily, the sergeant glared at the young woman in green.

Dye smiled, his eyes still on his captain. "Thank you, Sergeant. I don't think Captain Martigay will present much of a problem." He raised his eyebrows at her as she smiled back.

A commotion outside preceded a guard's hurried entry. "Sir," the guard announced breathlessly, "the Princess Bruthinia has just ridden in."

* * * * *

Without thinking, Martigay stood. "I should leave," she stated.

"Nay," Dye countered, standing abruptly. "Nay. Stay."

There was a rustle of expensive fabric as the Vandal princess swept into the room—just in time to find Dye and Martigay facing one another, separated by about a foot of breathless space.

The princess took in the situation at a glance. Taking the chair that Warrik offered, she slowly drew off her embroidered gloves. "At this point, Dye," she said, her voice a quiet threat, "I think it would be only polite for you to ask your lover to leave."

"I'm not his lover," Martigay said quickly.

"Captain Martigay was invited before I knew of your coming," Dye told the princess.

"You're embarrassing me, Dye." The princess's voice was a cold slice of quiet.

"I'd be embarrassing my captain if I asked her to leave. What are you doing here, Bruthinia?"

"Just keeping an eye on my interests." The princess stared coldly at Martigay.

"I'm not his lover," Martigay repeated.

The princess ignored her. "The king will be giving up a lot after he's wed," she announced in a voice like brittle ice.

At this announcement, Dye's eyes narrowed to a blaze of blue fire but his gaze never left Martigay's face, and he didn't take his seat again until his captain was back in her chair. A great deal of commotion ensued as the cook's assistants hurried to set a place and pour wine for the Vandal princess.

Unruffled, the elegant blonde ignored most of the people at the table, with whom she seemed to have been previously acquainted, and struck up a conversation with Davik's handsome brother. "You might be interested in checking out my new black, Warrik. She's descended from Morghan's Hoyden."

"Warrik's destroyer is from the Hoyden line as well," Davik pointed out.

The princess nodded as though this was common knowledge. "Through what dam?"

During dinner, the conversation centered around horses which led the princess to make the following suggestion. "Might I propose a race tomorrow to see which is the purer breed?"

Warrik laughed good-naturedly at the princess's arrogant insinuation, knowing his destroyer equal to any of Hoyden's line. "Ten gold?" he suggested as a wager.

"Is that the best you can come up with?" the princess returned in sultry pout.

Warrik raised both eyebrows.

"I propose a forfeit from the loser," she put forth suggestively. "The winner can make one demand of the loser...any demand," she continued, flirting ruthlessly with Warrik and ignoring the man to whom she was betrothed.

"How if I just ask for your horse, in forfeit?"

The princess shook her head. "You're disappointing me, Warrik. It can't be a material item like a horse, or jewelry, or gold."

"How if I asked for your Kingdom?"

"That's not mine to give as I don't rule—yet."

Warrik eyed Dye as his lips came together shrewdly. "Let's have it written down, then," he said as Dye stood to fetch a sheet of parchment from the table behind him. "Davik can hold the wagers," Warrik said, scratching out the agreement, "and we'll have Martigay, here, drop the flag to start the contest."

"My Lord," Martigay spoke up swiftly. "I don't think that would be —"

The king's electric blue eyes flared. "Humor my friend, Martigay."

"But, sir. Scarface can't bear to be behind another horse. He'll want to race too. He'll try to get out in front."

The princess laughed. "Well, if you're unable to manage your mount, he's welcome to eat our dust." Warrik tore the parchment in two and pushed one piece toward the princess for her signature. "Still, it's a shame you can't handle your horse."

Martigay's eyes cut to the princess and narrowed. "Yeah," she said. "Just like it's a shame stupidity isn't terminal. Thanks for the invitation."

There was a hitch in the princess's voice and she glared across the table at Martigay. "Of course the race's outcome will depend not only on the horse's speed, but on the rider's ability as well."

"Not to mention the rider's weight," Warrik interrupted in a drawl. "You have me at a disadvantage there, princess."

"Ganna Reean," the princess said, signing her name to the parchment then returning her gaze to Martigay. "Tough luck," she translated for the soldier's benefit. "I can speak seven different languages," she announced haughtily.

"Effing good for carthing malaka you," the soldier said under her breath.

"What was that?"

"I can curse in nine," Martigay returned pleasantly as Warrik snorted back an ill-advised laugh.

"Malaka," he recovered quickly. "Isn't that…Raithan?"

Dye stiffened beside her, caught her eye.

"I've a friend who's a Raith," she admitted.

"Brand." The word slipped out of Dye's mouth. "My Scout Captain," he filled in, his face tight.

"You have a Raith? I'd like to meet him," Warrik said.

"*You'd* like to meet him," the princess cut in. "*I'd* like to meet him." She returned her attention to Martigay. "Is it true what they say about Raithan men?"

Stonily, Martigay eyed her—as one would watch a snake.

"Their cocks are *huge* compared to other men's? They make better lovers?"

"I wouldn't *know* whether or not they make better lovers," Martigay replied, "not having *sampled* a large number of others. Perhaps *you'd* be the best judge of that."

The princess stood suddenly, her eyes lit with fury as she turned her gaze on Dye, clearly demanding his intervention. "I won't stand here and be insulted," she informed him, coldly.

"Then you have two choices," Dye pointed out in the ensuing silence. "You can either sit down…or you can leave. And let me warn you, Bruthinia," he added quietly, "you'll find there's a limit to how much the King of Thrall will give up for his wife, after he's wed. The respect due to him is *not* on the table."

With her own words thrown back in her face, the princess turned abruptly, her silk skirts swishing as she swept out through the inn's doors.

Warrik laughed outright and that got Davik started. And though his wife elbowed him in an attempt to quiet him, she soon joined in, as well. Only Dye remained quiet.

"Sorry," Martigay mumbled in his direction. "I didn't mean to insult her…very much."

Dye twirled his silver goblet between his fingers without looking at her. "So now you're friends with Brand," he said conversationally. "You only met him last week."

Petra caught back her laugh in mid-hiccup and stared at her brother.

"Warrik, here, knows something about Raiths." Dye turned his attention to the blond warrior. "He had a Raithan girl once. Didn't you tell me they only wed their own kind, Warrik?"

"That's usually the case," Warrik confirmed, with amused interest.

Dye smirked at Martigay as she received this information.

"They're a proud race," Warrik went on. "Think themselves better than others. The Raithan girl I knew wouldn't have wed me, though I was a Prince of Khal and she no more than the stable master's daughter. Raiths have no reservations, however, about whom they bed."

At this Martigay laughed. "Brand and I aren't *close* friends," she told him. "But I'll let you know if and when I find anything out." Dye nodded at the goblet, his jaw tight and hard. "I could use a good basis for comparison," she added with a grin of pure mischief.

He raised his eyes and his jaw softened to smile at her.

For many moments she basked in that smile. When the king smiled, it was like the sun coming out. What a lady-killer the guy was. Too bad he didn't take advantage of it—with her. She was in the mood to be taken advantage of—to be taken, period. So long as it was the king doing the taking.

"What's your plan to retake Amdahl?" Davik interrupted, as Dye's face turned serious. "A siege would hurt your people who are inside the walls as much as the Saharat occupying the city."

Dye nodded. "Nonetheless, my first objective is to take the mines. The Saharat will have a hard time paying for imported food without the gold. Hopefully, the populace will rise up and give us a hand when we get there. Maybe even get the gates open for us."

Warrik grimaced. "Sounds messy. I suppose your garrison there was wiped out?"

"Aye." Dye stopped to think. "I might be able to swim across at night and get up the walls before anyone got wind of me. I'd have some warning if anyone was about."

"Swim?" Martigay interjected.

Petra nodded. "The city is situated against the sea, its walls built close up to the river Donichal that splits to surround the city on its way to the ocean."

"That Raith in your scouts might be able to help you," Warrik suggested.

Dye shook his head. "He couldn't take me through the walls — he's not powerful enough. And I'd not ask a man to do something I could do."

"That was fair enough when you were a captain," Petra pointed out gently, "but you're the king now."

At this, the three men exchanged glances. "It would be ideal if we could get a man inside the walls," Warrik persevered. "I'll go with you, if you want to give it a try."

Dye shrugged as he returned his attention to the girl glancing anxiously over her shoulder. Catching her eye, he questioned her with a lifted eyebrow.

"I'd best be going," she murmured "It'll be dark soon."

Rising with her, Dye's gaze followed Martigay's departure.

Warrik's eyes lit up with amusement. "What are you sitting *there* for?" he prodded. "She said, herself, she needed a basis for comparison."

Petra nodded her agreement. "I think it's starting to rain," she commented innocently. "That dress is going to get ruined."

"Excuse me," Dye said, pushing back his chair and grabbing his cloak. The door closed behind him as his three guests grinned at each other.

Chapter Nine

"Martigay."

She turned, blinking in the gray, drizzling weather.

"Thank you...for having lastmeal with me." Dye stopped about a foot away from her, holding the cloak out toward her.

Her chin came up as she eyed him critically. "Are you really going to wed that...princess?" she asked.

"Nay," he said after a pause, "the king is going to wed that princess."

She nodded. Slowly, she smiled. "The king will be giving up a lot after he's wed."

He smiled back at her. "Aye. The king will be giving up a lot."

"Perhaps you could keep a little something on the side. The Queen wouldn't have to know about it."

"Are you volunteering?"

"Not at all. Just making a recommendation. Wouldn't want the king to lose his sanity."

It started to rain in earnest and still he held the cloak out to her. His lips ached and more than anything else in his life, he wanted a kiss—even more than he wanted a fuck and that surprised him.

The pour of rain transformed Martigay's hair into streaming curls and he followed the curls down over her shoulders with his eyes, stopping when he got to her chest. Her nipples stabbed at the wet green fabric as though fighting to get to him. Taking a step toward her, he wrapped the cloak around her shoulders.

And once he touched her, he was done for and he knew it. His hand snagged her behind the neck as he pulled her face to his and his lips slashed down on her open mouth. His other hand traveled to her face, shaking, as his thumb went under her jaw and his fingers furrowed into the hair behind her ear. As the rain turned into a downpour, he twisted his lips on hers at the same time that he maneuvered her backward beneath a tree, pressing her into its trunk. Gulping in a breath of air and rain, his head angled to turn his mouth on her lush lips.

With one hand capturing the back of her skull and the other holding her face, he felt her chin tremble beneath his thumb and he thrust his tongue between her lips to enter her shuddering mouth and scrape over the tongue that shivered against his own. Knowing the little minx fought for control inflamed his senses and his body responded with unreasonable excitement. When her fingers tugged at the hand that bracketed her face, he tightened his grip, unwilling to surrender his hold on her. He felt her other hand grip his hip more tightly and then the yank on his wrist again. Cursing into her mouth, he let her have the damn hand.

She pulled it to her breast.

Moaning his gratitude into her mouth, he crushed his body into hers. The heel of his hand was beneath the warm handful of her breast, his fingers scraping up to cage the taut nipple, his cock pressed into her smooth, warm belly as the thick mound of her rise pressed back, seeking his long ridge of his cock.

Pushing his hand into the open décolletage of the dress, his thumb and forefinger drew together over the chamois-soft skin of her breast as he sought out and found her stiff, upright nipple. Rolling the rough bud of flesh between his fingers, he tugged at it as she gasped into his mouth, and his dick jerked in response to the captivating sound of female arousal.

Taking that sound as an invitation to proceed, again he tugged, a little roughly, as though her body was his to command, his to possess—his alone. And Hadi help the man who *ever* tried to take his place at her breast.

Simultaneously, lightning flashed and thunder cracked ten paces to the right and he jumped away from her. Together, they blinked breathlessly at the smoking column of steam produced by the vaporized rain.

Gasping for breath, Martigay watched the rain plaster Dye's hair against his head and mold his clothes to his perfect body. When he shook his head, straight streamers of wet fire flew around his face.

"I need to get you out from under this tree," he rasped, staring at her like he wanted to eat her whole.

"We could continue this," she offered breathlessly, "in my tent."

His eyes were the color found at the hard edge of lightning and they burned through the rain at her. "I'm wedding the Vandal princess," he stated in a flat voice made sharp with determination.

"Oh, come on, Dye! It's not like I'm trying to steal you from Bruthinia. I just want to borrow you for a while."

Staring at her, he shook his head. "You deserve more than this. More than a man...who's going to wed...Bruthinia." He shuddered in the cold slash of rain.

She watched the hard lines of rain batter the lean edges of his handsome face and smiled. "After you're wed, you could always...imagine it's someone else."

He nodded at her. "I'd have to," he said morosely.

Laughing at him, she tugged the cloak closed around her as he pulled her out from beneath the tree.

"Come on, Captain Martigay, I'll walk you back to your tent."

Not the least bit anxious to get back to her tent where she'd have to give up the arm that wrapped across her back and gripped her shoulder, Martigay dragged her feet through the sloppy puddles, careless of the fact that she was ruining the soft leather slippers she'd borrowed from the king's trunk. The wet, chilling weather was excuse enough to pull in close against his side.

"Why fight the inevitable, Dye? We're going to make love."

"We are *not* going to make love," he said, cutting her with his eyes. "Although," he muttered, "I may lay you once or twice, just to get you out of my system."

The woman was hopelessly naïve if she thought they would make love when—*if*—they got together. It wouldn't be like that. It would just be sex. Hard, intense, brutal, grinding sex. Sex wasn't something he wanted to do *with* her. It was something he wanted to do *to* her.

He'd have her if he could. He'd take her—hard. When it came to sex, he was passionate about the subject. Violently passionate. He wanted to take the proud little vixen—take her and break her in bed. Break down her confident, cool reserve and hear her helpless cries, her whispered demands for more, her hoarse screams for completion—uttered in raw, uninhibited passion.

It was a struggle to fight the overwhelming urge to give into passionate savagery—and take her. That was why his hand had shaken, earlier, when he had held her face and taken the kiss. It had taken that much effort to rein in the passion she evoked in him.

She shook her head. "You're wrong, Dye. We're going to make love."

"Not tonight," he told her, stopping outside her tent.

The warm glow from inside her shelter almost demanded that he join her. The thought of their bodies twisted together in the golden glow of light while she watched with open eyes, his body over hers, his cock rubbing against the delicate silk of her skin, his shaft sliding into her pussy as he rose on stiff arms above her, was almost enough to make him spill right there and then.

But at the same time, that warm, revealing glow would betray them both, he reminded himself. And the shadows that rose to move on the tent's walls would be testimony to a king's weakness as well as proof of a royal princess dishonored.

Knowing he'd regret it, knowing his body could hardly afford to be pushed even a small inch closer to climax—to her—he, nonetheless, couldn't resist pulling her body against his, his right hand spreading to hold the left cheek of her bottom. As he did so, his mind was tormented by the memory of the girl, last night in the inn, her legs pushed open and spread wide on the stool, her cunt spilling for him, her shimmering wet slit a shuddering open flame begging to be fucked.

If he didn't pull away now, he realized, he never would. At the same time, he prayed for her touch on the thick width of his shaft.

Somehow, she got her hand between their bodies, and his prayer was answered when she palmed him roughly at the ties. He let her, unwilling to stop her, pulling away only enough to watch her stroke the thick ridge that threatened to break through his laces and overfill her small hand. Hungry for her touch on his cock, unable to deny himself, he allowed her rough treatment of his doeskin-covered cock. Rain pattered at his back and worked its way under his collar to trickle down his spine as, resting his forehead on the crown of her head, he let her stroke him to within an inch of satisfaction, only pulling away when she started to tug at his ties.

"That's enough," he rasped in a raw voice. And it was. On the verge of spilling, he backed away, his fists clenching on empty air as he let the pelting rain fill the space between them.

"Your cloak," she reminded him, shrugging the heavy wool off one shoulder.

But he shook his head, sodden strands of scarlet whipping his cheeks. "Get inside," he ordered her. "You can return it tomorrow." With these words, and his eyes on the pale, beckoning curve of her shoulder, he forced himself backward a few more steps before he finally turned away.

When he'd put a hundred paces between them, he stopped to lean his burning forehead against the cool stone of a small shed, unlacing his ties with shaking hands. The hut's wide eaves sheltered him from the slash of rain as, sliding down to his knees and spreading his legs, he took his cock in hand.

Five pumps later he had forced himself. Body taut, eyes blinking, he watched his semen fly from his cock head to make shining lines of dripping silver on the gray stone. Depleted and drained, he stared at the wall's rough surface, wishing it were — instead — the sweet, smooth skin of Martigay's upturned ass.

Unsatisfied and edgy, Dye breathed out a curse for the circumstances that had placed him here, alone in a dark corner of a dismal night, pumping his cock instead of thrusting between a woman's legs and experiencing the fuck due a man — due a king.

He groaned as he stared down at the ruddy, used flesh in his hand. How could he have thought one woman as good as the next — when he'd signed that wedding contract? *How could he have known otherwise?*

A lifetime of eager and available women had never given him reason to think anything else. And Martigay was just as eager and available as all the others! What was it about the proud, arrogant...bold, daring...defiant, insolent — but the Vandal princess was proud enough if that was the attraction.

He shook his head. The princess was haughty and cold — cold to her roots. She lacked the warmth and fire Martigay kept bottled up inside that laughing exterior — the fire he'd glimpsed every time she'd challenged his authority. He didn't get hard for the princess — even when she was standing next to him! Whereas the mere thought of Martigay had the blood racing from every extremity to pound its way into his cock.

Feeling wrung out and worn, Dye pushed his cock inside his leggings, pulled himself together and stumbled back to the inn. The door banged against the wall as he pushed inside the long room, where only Petra remained to greet him. Davik and his brother had each retired to one of the two pavilion tents outside. Shaking the rain out of his hair, he stalked across the room, ignoring the question in his sister's eyes.

But Petra wouldn't let it go that easily. "You finally find a woman who doesn't bore you?"

Rubbing a small blanket through his hair, Dye turned to frown at his sister. "Don't meddle, Petra." His sister looked disappointed. "I can't read her," he offered reluctantly.

"What?"

"I can't read her. Can't sense her feelings." He smiled wryly. "Here am I, a man who can learn the feelings of anyone I choose—except for the one person I'm…curious about. It's like her feelings are shuttered from me."

"Perhaps that's the attraction. She's a mystery."

"Perhaps."

"Perhaps she *has* no feelings," Petra joked.

Dye answered this with a wry smile.

Petra was thoughtful. "Do you think…she has Slurian blood? Like us?"

"There's no reason to think so. I've always been able to pick up *your* feelings."

"Aye, but I'm different from you. While I have the Westerman night vision and the Slurian ability to physically touch others with my mind, I can't sense others' feelings as you can. If she's like you, she might be able to block her feelings…or read yours for that matter."

Dye smiled grimly. "I certainly hope she can't read mine."

"Oh?"

"Because I'm pretty much thinking only one thing when I'm around her."

"She wouldn't have to be Slurian to figure that out, Dye."

"Nay?" he asked quietly.

"Nay. So why don't you—"

"I'm wedding Bruthinia."

Petra's mouth tightened in irritation. "A political wedding," she said softly. "That's a mistake, Dye."

"A peace accord with Vandaland will save a thousand lives every year. How can you call that a mistake?"

"A year ago, I'd not have argued with you, Dye. As little interest as you've ever shown in a woman, I'd have thought Bruthinia would do as well as anyone else. But now..." she sighed. "Give up the throne to one of our cousins and let someone else wed Bruthinia."

"Can you think of any of them who would have her?"

"Not offhand. Does she...have any sisters? Any sisters a little less unpleasant?"

Dye was silent, his thoughts obviously not on Bruthinia.

"Are you in love with her?"

Dye laughed, frustration edging the sound. "How would *I* know?"

Petra nodded with a sigh. Although her brother had never lacked for female company, she knew he'd never met a woman who interested him in the least.

Some women might have called her brother ruggedly handsome, but the cliché fell short of describing the man standing before her. Dye could only be described as *dangerously* handsome. The long line of his body was like a mean whip, corded and wrapped with wiry strength that bunched and stretched as he moved. His hard face lacked anything that could be mistaken for tenderness. He'd left that in a distant past—a past in which their youngest brother had lived...and died. The lines that etched his cheeks, either side of his mouth, were almost cruel when a smile was not present—and he was a man who rarely smiled. The black tattoo slashing through his left eyebrow fixed his expression into a permanent, measuring frown.

"She's like that river we grew up next to. During the spring rush. She's wild, unpredictable. It's breathtaking, overwhelming. She's...a shock. A shock to my system," he finally admitted.

"Sounds to me like she's just what you need. I know you don't normally fraternize with your troops, Dye, but perhaps you should make an exception in this case."

Dye straightened with a sigh, and turned his back on his sister. "The wedding contract is signed…" he said with a tone of finality, "signed weeks ago."

"When is the wedding to take place?" she asked him.

"Upon a resolution in the south. The binding ceremony will take place in the Palace at Amdahl, after we've regained it." Dye blew out a breath. "Until then, Bruthinia will be Thrall's guest in the Palace at Tharran."

Petra smiled grimly. "You could always let the Saharat keep Amdahl."

Dye nodded. "If the contract isn't honored, the Vandals will take it as an insult. It will mean out and out war."

And he wouldn't do that. He wouldn't break his promise of wedding and risk what would surely turn into a long, bloody conflict with Vandaland. He wouldn't risk the lives of his countrymen. He'd give up the throne first.

And it was down to that—either give up the girl or dishonor his contract and walk away from the leadership his grandmother had entrusted to him.

Chapter Ten

"Keep your little mongrel away from my breed."

Martigay's head came around as though she'd been slapped.

Dressed in orange silk and mounted on her black mare, the princess snarled down at Martigay and her little stallion. "The mare's coming into season. This animal is descended from Hoyden. I don't want your stunted little wretch of a stud fucking things up." With a flick of its black tail, the princess's mare put her legs beneath her, and both mare and mistress were away.

Scarface snorted and tossed his head as Martigay leaned forward to pat his neck. "You needn't act so innocent," she muttered. "That's exactly what you had in mind. And don't bother trying to deny it." Together they watched the mare's back end move away, tail provocatively lifting and switching. Scarface neighed at the receding black rump and she laughed at him. "Of course she likes you. You may not be tall, but you more than make up for it with your huge...spots. Mind your manners, Romeo. We have to drop the flag."

Circling away, she put the inn between herself and the two blacks before approaching them from the other side of the building. The race was to take place on the muddy track outside the inn, from the door of the inn to a point a half league distant.

Dye's army lined the road to watch, while the king and his royal guests waited at the distant finish point. A word from Martigay halted the paint while she pulled out the red scarf tucked into her jerkin. It fluttered on the breeze for two instants before she let it fall. In the next moments, she was fighting to rein back her pony as the blacks took off.

Dragging the paint's head around, Martigay forced the pony into a tight circle—but he came out of it like a tightly coiled spring and shot toward the spray of mud that followed the racing horses. Initially fighting for control, she eventually gave in with a laugh and let the pony run, moving her weight forward and hunching over his withers as he streaked forward in an exhilarating burst of speed. Reveling in the ride, in the power of the beast between her legs, Martigay laughed into the wind that rushed at her face and whipped her hair back to dance like a banner on the air.

By now the two royal breeds had what was probably an insurmountable lead on the pony and Martigay couldn't help but laugh as the paint stretched to catch them, eating up the ground at a courageous pace as he pursued the two black rumps in the distance—his interest centered more on *one rump* than the other, Martigay had to assume.

At first she teased him. "Never on your best day, Scarface. Never on your best day are you going to catch that royal black ass." The pony forged forward and Martigay watched the separating distance between them diminish. Leaning over her mount's neck, she whispered in its ear. "Did you hear what she called you, Scarface? She called you a mongrel."

The pony leapt a running ditch and carried on.

Now they inched up alongside Warrik's stallion, the destroyer's huge lungs bellowing as it labored to keep its place just behind the mare, the mud from the mare's heels flying back to splatter the pursuing riders.

Within scent of the breeding mare, the little stallion jetted forward. Crouched up against the pony's neck, Martigay peeked up long enough to catch a glimpse of the mare's lifted tail. Based on this evidence, she had to conclude the mare's heart wasn't so much in winning the race as in losing it—to one of the stallions bearing down on her—and the sooner the better. Frisking and skittering just ahead, the mare maintained her lead for several racing steps, while Martigay saw a short whip appear in Bruthinia's hand to smack against the mare's flank.

At that signal, the royal black mare stuttered in its long stride, skidding on the muddy road. At the same time, Scarface bolted forward as though the sharp bite of the whip had seared his own flanks.

A burst of phenomenal speed, a blur of black, a flash of brilliant orange silk, and the princess and her royal mount were behind Martigay and her pony. Scarface raced for the finish point, the blacks' thundering hooves slapping and pounding ineffectually behind the little stallion as the crowd at the finish point blossomed large with a raucous cheer of approval then disappeared behind them.

Easing the cantering pony to a halt, Martigay slid from the horse's back and tugged to loosen the girth rope, yanking at the saddlebow as the pony walked away from beneath his saddle. "She's all yours, Scarface. Go get her."

Dragging the saddle along on her hip, she came up behind the princess, who was engaged in a heated argument with the big Khallic prince.

"But there wasn't a winner!" the princess maintained as she followed the big man to where his brother stood. Warrik held out his hand and Davik put the two folded agreements into it.

"The paint won the race," Warrik was telling the princess, opening one of the agreements, and scanning the document with his eyes.

"But the girl didn't wager!"

Warrik regarded the fragment of parchment and shook his head. "It says here the loser of the race owes a forfeit to the winner." With that, he handed the two pieces of parchment to the startled soldier.

The princess opened her mouth to protest but Warrik cut her off. "Where I come from, princess, wagers are *always* met. We Khals never renege on a bet." Smiling at the young soldier, he winked. "I await your pleasure, Captain Martigay."

The princess turned away with a scream.

Then screamed again to find the scruffy, unkempt little stallion mounting her royal black. The stallion's teeth were set in the saddlebow of the black's fine leather saddle as the mare's back legs buckled into a crouch and she backed her hindquarters to meet the mottled shaft that sought her entrance. With eyes rolled backward into her head, the mare stilled in shivering acceptance, waiting to take the stallion's heaving thrust.

* * * * *

"Have you demanded your forfeit from the princess?" Pall asked Martigay later that day.

Martigay shrugged. "The lady doesn't have anything I want."

"You could ask her to kiss your ass."

Martigay winced in the middle of a grin. "Somehow that doesn't seem very appealing."

"You could ask her to kiss *my* ass," Pall put to her cheerfully as Martigay responded with a crooked smile. "And while you're at it, you could get her to shag me, as well."

Martigay grinned suspiciously at him. "You fancy the princess?"

Pall shrugged. "She's a looker."

"That's all she is," Martigay grunted. "Setting your sights a bit high, aren't you?"

"Speak for yourself, Martigay. You're not the only ambitious soldier in this army."

"I'll give your suggestion some thought," she told him. "Right now I'm playing with the idea of telling her to go to Hadi's."

"Can you get there from here?" Pall inquired with a lazy, philosophical air.

Martigay nodded. "It's west of here. Way, *way* west. Overseas, I think. I'll draw her a map," Martigay said lightly. "And she can spend the rest of her life trying to find it."

Chapter Eleven

"What is it about women and horses?" With these words to Warrik, Dye slid a glance sideways at Martigay.

Just for a chance to get out and ride, he'd joined a unit he was sending north to meet a supply train. Two of his messengers accompanied him, one of whom was Martigay. When Warrik had found Dye saddling his mount, the big blond had insisted on tagging along.

Warrik grinned at his friend as he considered his answer. Turning in his saddle to rest a hand on his destroyer's rump, he took a good, long look at Dye's Captain of Messengers—riding about twenty paces distant on their right.

"Your captain is fond of her pony?"

Dye nodded. "Uncommonly fond."

Warrik grinned. "That little leather saddle of hers fits her like a glove." Dye frowned at the grinning Khal and Warrik laughed at him. "I have it on good authority that a woman can come while in the saddle—riding."

Dye turned stunned eyes on his friend. "You're yanking my chain," he said flatly.

Warrik shook his head. "When a woman spreads her legs in the saddle, the horse's girth is enough to part the lips between her legs. Add a nice, well-fitting, smooth leather saddle and—" Warrik shrugged with a grin.

"No." Dye leaned forward in his saddle to view Martigay and found her returning his gaze. "No," he repeated uncertainly.

"She's been watching you all morning," Warrik pointed out.

Dye frowned at the giant blond. "No," he repeated. "Without…?"

"…touching herself?" Slowly, slyly, Warrik nodded.

"You're not serious. You're messing with me."

Warrik laughed. "Five gold says we can make her come."

Dye considered his friend uncertainly. "How would we know? If she did?"

"We'll know," Warrik declared with confidence.

Although the morning was brisk, the late winter sun was bright and shone down to warm Warrik's chest after he pulled off his doeskin jerkin, bundled it into a ball, tossed it at Dye and wrapped his reins loosely around the pommel of his saddle. The sun was almost in the middle of the sky as he leaned back, closed his eyes, and rested his hands just behind his saddle on the black's rump. The horse's gait lifted his hips in an undulating motion that was more than suggestive.

Dye watched Martigay while continuing his conversation with his friend. More than once, she glanced their way while the horses plodded on at a steady pace and her pony's gait rocked her body like a loosely fluttering wave. Dye shook his head with a snort when Warrik tossed his head, shaking out his thick gold mane and then running a big hand back through his hair.

"How am I doing?" he asked Dye with a wink.

"You're an idiot, man."

"By now, Northman, you should know better than to insult me."

They continued on about a half league before Warrik shifted as though he were uncomfortable, stretching his huge tiger-like frame to clasp both his hands behind his neck. Slowly, he turned his upper body—first to the left, then right—before he unwound his arms and reached for the ties at his groin.

Dye snorted. "What are you doing, now?"

"Getting comfortable," Warrik explained easily. "Is she watching?"

"Aye...no...aye."

Slowly, lazily, Warrik pulled on his ties to loosen them. "Still watching?"

"Aye."

Warrik stretched lazily, hooking the top edge of his doeskins with his thumb and dragging the breeks away from his body and down. Despite himself, Dye began to laugh. "Fuck me, Warrik. You're crazy!"

Warrik returned an easy grin. "She still watching?"

"Aye," Dye laughed. "Everyone's watching! You're making a fucking spectacle of yourself."

"Good," he returned. "Now it's your turn."

"What!"

"I'm just the warm-up act. You're the main attraction."

Reining in his mount, Warrik turned the black's head to come up behind, then alongside Dye's mount, to position Dye between himself and the girl. "Get rid of that vest and jerkin," he told him. "No. Take your time, you ignorant, northern barbarian. Don't you know anything about women?"

In answer, Dye shot vest and jerkins at the big man's face as Warrik caught the clothing easily. "Now rub your hands down your thighs," Warrik suggested, his eyes on the woman across the way.

"What for?"

Warrik pretended a sigh. "Try to work with me, here, Dye. Just do it."

Shifting in his saddle, Dye dragged his hands down the tops of his thighs as he watched Warrik's eyes on the girl.

"Oh yeah," Warrik breathed in appreciation, "she likes that."

"Why? What's she doing?"

Warrik ignored the King of Thrall. "Now, stand up in the stirrups and adjust your—"

"Aye, man. Aye. I get it. I don't need to be told everything." With his weight on his feet in the stirrups, Dye adjusted the doeskin that bunched in his crotch, which, by that time, needed adjusting. Dropping back into the saddle, he tugged at the front of his ties as though making himself comfortable. Wrapping his reins around the pommel on his saddle, he then reached up with both hands to push his long fingers back through the silken fire of his hair.

Warrik chuckled quietly. "You should see this," he said in a low voice. "She can't take her eyes off you." The big blond sighed contentedly. "And all the time, that pony keeps up that steady rocking pace. I'll bet she's creaming for you right now. I'll bet she's about one inch away from arrival."

Dye pulled in his bottom lip with his tongue. "She's not the only one," he muttered.

"No! Don't look at her or she'll be onto us in an instant."

"What next, then?"

"Just keep it up," Warrik advised, "while we edge our horses over toward her."

"And why are we doing that?"

Warrik fought to snuff out his chuckle of amusement. "I want to see her eyes, see if they're glazing yet."

Dye glanced back at the fifty mounted men who followed them and got a quick look at Martigay when his eyes were on the way back. Her wide eyes were fixed on his upper body. Without thinking, he flexed his biceps and Warrik laughed outright.

"Okay," Warrik said, almost strangling on his laughter. "Okay…timing is everything…I count to ten and you turn around and smile at her. You remember how to smile? Ready? On my count."

It came about just as Warrik had predicted. At the count of ten, Dye turned toward her. Dipping his chin, he lifted his gaze to rest on her at the same time that he let the corners of his mouth kick up in a smile—then breathlessly watched her reaction as the smile unwound on his face. Her eyes were wide on his for an instant, then they half-closed and her mouth opened as her head jerked back and her body wavered and flickered like a flame.

"*Fuck me!*" Warrik whispered, awestruck. "Isn't that beautiful? Wouldn't you like to have that on your dick right about now? Wrapped around your cock like a wet flame?" Dye stifled a groan as he dragged his wrist over his ties. "Told you we'd know," Warrik reminded his friend.

Dye tried to swallow through a dry throat as he watched Martigay's eyes open at the end of a shudder. Her cheeks were pink and her eyes huge on his as she dragged her bottom lip through her teeth and averted her eyes. Dye's eyebrows came together. "She's embarrassed," he told himself quietly. "We've embarrassed the girl."

Warrik shrugged. "She'll get over it."

Concerned, Dye watched as Martigay spurred her horse ahead of them.

"What's she up to?" Warrik asked with suspicion.

"She's just trying to get away," Dye told him, troubled.

Drawing her mount to a sudden halt just ahead of them, the woman swung from the pony's back to stand beside the beast. Bending over double, ostensibly to inspect the beast's fetlock — she presented the perfect heart of her bottom for their profound appreciation.

"The little minx!" Warrik roared with laughter. "Embarrassed, my ass," he chortled as the two men kicked their mounts into a trot to catch up to her.

As they approached, she continued her charade, running her hand up the pony's cannon, testing its leg between fetlock and knee. She straightened and turned as the men came alongside her. The little tease had loosened the ties at her chest and both men could see right down into her fabulous cleavage.

93

"Everything all right, Captain Martigay?" Dye choked out bravely, forcing himself to drag his eyes out of her cleavage and lift them to her face.

"Just checking my mount, sir," she answered. "His gait seemed a little…unsettling. And a woman has to be cautious when she's only her horse to rely on." She glanced down at the horse's leg then back up. "But I'm satisfied…now." Swinging back into the saddle, she raced back to join the ranks while Dye fought the urge to follow her with his eyes.

"That little chit's asking for it," Warrik pointed out, his eyes lit with amusement as well as admiration. "Why don't you give it to her?"

"I can't," Dye told him with stoic determination. "Though Mithra knows I'd like too. And that's not the worst of it," he rasped. "I'm as hard as a rock. I'm going to be fucking blue in about an hour."

Warrik shook his head. "No, that's not the worst of it," he said with a grin. "The worst of it is—you owe me five gold."

Chapter Twelve

Dye's eyes scanned the message quickly before he grabbed up a quill and scrawled a response then stood to call for a messenger. Ducking outside the inn, he came face to face with Martigay. He blinked—a startled, uneasy moment. Stepping around her, he thrust the message into Donal's hand. "Get this to Greegor, *now*," he spat out the short, terse order. Turning back to his tent, his eyes connected with hers again for a brief instant. He broke the connection as he brushed back through the inn's door.

She followed him in and he shook his head as he heard her steps on the wooden floor, behind him. Shields firmly in place, he turned to face her.

"What in Hadi's name was that about?" she rasped in a low snarl.

With his eyes, he dared her to push him.

"That message was mine! I was next in line for the next outgoing message. What in Hadi's name is Donal doing carrying *my* message!"

Dye stared at her silently, jaw grinding, an eruption brewing in the wild volcanic blue of his eyes. "The message was…important," he grated out. "Vital."

For an instant she looked stunned, angry, hurt. "*What!* I'm not good enough to carry an important message? I'm not fast enough? There isn't a *horse* in your army faster than Scarface. There isn't a rider in your army who can outdistance *me*!"

"*The assignment was dangerous*!" he exploded.

She took a step toward him. "I should be carrying that message. I was next in line. Why the—!"

His hands shot toward her as he clamped her upper arms and lifted her body until her face was level with his. "You want to know why?" he snarled. "This is why!" He jerked her forward and his lips connected with hers for a brief instant as he slammed her into the nearest wall and, grabbing her hand, forced it beneath his ties. "And that!"

Still reeling from the intense shock of his lips, given and almost immediately withdrawn, Martigay stammered when she felt his hand locking hers around the steel-hard length of his shaft. "Wha...what are you doing?"

"Don't you know? Keep thinking, Captain Martigay. It will come to you."

"Nothing's coming," she grunted defensively, struggling in his iron grasp.

"Nay?" Releasing his hold on her, he thrust his hand into her leggings. With his body pinning hers to the wall, she felt a thick finger part her labia with an expert flick. "How about now? Need another hint, Martigay? Then let me spell it out for you. I want to fuck you before you die."

Martigay quit struggling as she stared into the blue eyes that burned inches from her own. "Before I die?"

"Before you die — carrying a message to Greegor, the message warning him of the Saharat force amassing in the south and marching north to divide our forces, the message which may or may not reach him in time — especially when there's more than an odds-on chance that you'd be killed by enemy riders on your way there!"

"Saharat!" she stuttered, "In the south? Where did they come from?"

"Where do Saharat usually come from? From the desert!"

"They're not all in Amdahl?"

"Apparently not!"

"But —" Martigay stared at his face. "You...you can't do that! You can't show me favoritism. I'll lose face — respect. The men will snicker behind my back and hate me for it."

"I can do whatever I choose, soldier. I'm the Commander of this Army as well as the *fucking king*!"

Martigay swallowed as she stared into Dye's hard, amazonite gaze. "Well, get on with it, then. Let's see what a king can do."

Her invitation set him back for an instant. But only an instant. "Well, that's a reversal of position, Captain Martigay."

"Are you asking me to turn around?"

Despite the passion firing his limbs and accumulating in a stark rush for his dick, Dye couldn't stop the smile that crept over his mouth. He knew his eyes crinkled at the edges as he choked out the next sentence. "I'm asking why the sudden change of heart—about my favoritism."

Martigay shook her head. "I haven't changed my mind, sir—I still don't want special treatment."

"Thanks," he grunted harshly. "So you're assuming sex with me would be something less than special."

"No! No! Not at all, sir. I just consider this a slight detour…from my principles."

"Isn't that convenient," he pointed out in a rasp.

"Yes, sir," she admitted. "But, if you're going to get wet, you might as well go swimming."

"Are you wet, Captain Martigay?" he whispered against her ear. "Are you as wet as you were on your horse, yesterday?"

"See for yourself," she breathed in an inviting whisper of sound.

His finger slipped through her folds toward her vagina, and she blinked several times before his finger came to a halt at her opening. Her free hand smoothed over his hard forearm and slipped down to cover his hand as she rubbed his palm against her mons. "Dive in, sir."

"Don't tempt me, Martigay," he warned her with a frayed voice, "or you'll find my cock wedged so deep in your cunt you'll be tasting saltwater at the back of your throat."

Her only answer was a low, breathless moan which fired his limbs and thickened the long, steely length of his dick. Her small, female sounds of longing drove him to masculine need nothing short of brutal as he was almost overcome with the urge to thrust and fill and complete himself inside this woman.

The barrier of his ties loosened as she fumbled at his strings, then his cock was pushing through the opening she'd breeched. Her small hand wrapped around his cock again and he gasped. He had half a mind to forge up into her—there and then—but held back, wary of the cool challenge in her smoke-blue eyes, the steel composure with which she maintained a dignity at odds with the short, excited breaths that dampened her parted lips. Instead, he dipped his middle finger into her well and pulled the wet finger all the way through her folds to the top of her cleft. And dipped again. At the same time, she pumped at the loose skin covering the bow of his erection.

He kept his eyes on hers, watching them intently while her eyes remained focused on his. He continued to play in and out of her opening, up and through her folds, circling her clitoris then back down again to her vagina.

Her face remained expressionless as she continued to manhandle his dick with a brutal grip. Gritting his teeth, determined to win this contest of reserve, Dye waited for some kind of sign—thought her folds thickened, softened, but wasn't certain, kept playing his finger through her sex as it became increasingly difficult to concentrate with that tight little grip on his shaft urging an excited reaction out of his cock. Finally, he returned to her opening to find it running hot and wet, spilling over his fingers.

Pausing there to catch at the sweet running moisture with three fingers, he explored her slit, pushing her labia open and rubbing her clit with his flattened palm while his fingers deepened their intrusion into her cunt.

Confident that she was on the edge of orgasm and a wild, thrashing victory was at hand, his chest tightened in anticipation and his breath came in rough bursts as he rushed her forward, his eyes on hers, determined to witness the instant when she lost control, committed to remaining hard in her grip through her last internal shudder. Certain her defeat was within his grasp, he watched her face carefully as he shot two fingers deep inside her cunt at the same time that he gave her a small, vicious smile of triumph.

For an instant, her eyes lost their focus, half-closed, then blinked open to stare at him helplessly. In that instant, a storm of passion swirled in her smoke-blue eyes. And in that instant, he wanted her more than he'd ever wanted anything. Wanted her — helplessly female, defeated by lust, shafted on his cock and staring into his eyes as he fucked her — a slave to his cock.

But before he could get inside her, she lost it. Completely lost it. Her hand tightened around his shaft and her head went back as her body convulsed in shuddering jerks and her vagina clamped to hug his fingers as her release slid into his palm.

"Fuck," his voice scratched out of a dry throat as his cock thickened and stretched until he thought he would burst out of his skin. With gritted teeth he fought to ignore the hand that clamped and jerked uncontrollably on his dick as he continued the smooth motion of his fingers in and out of her cunt, continued to serve her need uninterrupted, the surface of his palm sliding inside the slick space between her spread labia.

Eventually, she opened her eyes to gaze at him. His hand was still inside her spread pussy while he savored the wet heat in his palm, holding her with a strong, still grip as her sex continued to close on his fingers in recurring tremors of aftershock. Her wide eyes on his were sleepy with satisfaction — and he fought to get inside her.

Overcharged and ready to spill at the least provocation, he tore at her ties and yanked at the top of her leggings, dragging them down over her hips. His cock rubbed into her wet cleft as his hips moved instinctively. Flexing his knees, he drove upward, missing the mark, grinding up through the clinging line of her sex that hugged his cock head in a sweet, carnal kiss and accelerated him toward orgasm. With her wet kiss sucking

Madison Hayes

at his sensitive cock head, he exploded, spilling into the dewy hair of her mound, pulling her lower body close and tight as his shaft jerked between their bodies and spat his ejaculate to coat their groins and seal their bodies together—naked cock to warm, felted pussy. Her groan was in his ear as she tried, too late, to climb onto his dick.

"You missed the mark," she murmured with a whimper of disappointment.

Nestling his face into the sheltering waves of her hair, he moaned a wet breath in answer, feeling empty and incomplete. "You're driving me mad," he told her.

"You need to get this out of your system," she told him between breaths. "You can't let your...interest in me interfere with my duties as a soldier. If you want to lay me before you have to expose me to danger, then I suggest you get on with it, sir, so that I can get on with my career."

"I can't do that," he said, realizing how close he'd come to violating his principles. "I can't do either," he confessed, "lay you or expose you to danger. Though Mithra knows I'd like to. Lay you," he clarified with a whisper, "and perhaps even expose you," he added, gruffly. "But not to danger."

With his hands on her waist, he eased her to the floor and took a step back, shaking his head at the same time.

"But you're right," he muttered after a long pause. His eyes were on the ground as he shook his head. "I've a war to win, an army to command, twelve thousand lives for which I'm responsible. I can't— You're right," he said looking back up at her. "I'm moving you out of the messengers."

"Sir!"

"You'll be joining my personal guard."

"But...the Royal Guard is Thrallish."

"You'll be a welcome addition. The guard could use some color and you're the right height."

"But...your guard has a captain."

100

He nodded again. "I'm sorry. You'll have to settle for sergeant." Turning from her, he rummaged on his desk before he found a red ribbon. Turning back to face her, he held the ribbon toward her.

Without realizing it, she shuffled a few steps backward. "*Sergeant!*"

"You'll look good in red," he told her, his face grim but determined. "Look on the bright side, Martigay. No one will be able to accuse you of favoritism."

Staring at the red ribbon, she shook her head as she backed up another step, unable to understand how he could do this to her—again. After…after she'd proven herself in her role as Captain of his Messengers and despite the rough, incomplete intimacy they'd shared several times now. Despite the warm, promising kiss beneath the tree just the other evening. The kiss cut short by the untimely bolt of lightning.

Her eyes burned with an aching pressure and she knew they'd soon fill. Sucking in her cheeks, she blinked at the ribbon then turned for the door.

"I've not dismissed you, Martigay."

Ignoring this, she continued pushing toward the door. She wouldn't let the bastard see her cry.

"Martigay! You go out that door and you go out it a pawyn."

Without hesitation, she drew her short steel from her belt and cut the ribboned braid close to her scalp. Her back was stiff as she flung the plaited twist of hair to the floor.

"Shit!" Dye cursed in the empty room. "Shit!" For several instants he stared at the long, dark braid on the floor—Martigay's shining hair twisted together with a single ribbon of blue—before he made his way across the room to pick it up.

Chapter Thirteen

He should be pleased, Dye reasoned.

He should be pleased.

Donal's message had reached Greegor in time for his lieutenant to race his troops east, joining Dye ahead of the Saharat advance. Upon Greegor's arrival, Dye had consolidated his lines, pulling his army together to camp in a wide band on the east bank of the Neelae River, firmly wedged between the Saharat advance and the forces occupying the city. After establishing the new base, he had sent a force of two thousand north to take the mines, thereby cutting off the main source of income that supported the Saharat trespassers inside the city — the cash they'd need to pay for the imported food and supplies Amdahl was largely dependant upon.

The mines had been taken without a fight, the small caretaking force of Saharat pelting off to the west before his advance. His men were currently searching those hills and woods in an effort to clear them of any loose bands that might hang around long enough to cause trouble.

The Saharat force approaching from the south and numbering about five thousand would have been more than enough to wipe out Greegor's unit, but shouldn't present much of a threat when they caught up to Dye's main force — if they were foolish enough to attack without a supporting force from Amdahl. The real danger lay in the prospect of the southern force being joined by the Saharat army in the city, leaving the safety of their walls to attack him at the same time. In this case, though the armies would be fairly evenly matched, Dye's army would be caught between the two forces and the Saharat would have a definite advantage that wouldn't be easily surmounted.

Still, all in all, he should be pleased.

He had Martigay close to him at all times, where he could be certain of her safety. And the thought that she was safe should have been a warming one. It might have been, had she not been so cold and distant. In the past several days, Martigay hadn't once looked at him, hadn't once smiled in his presence, hadn't once breathed any other words to him other than "Yes, sir".

She'd been angry with him before, but never like this. Never with such accompanying glacial frigidity. Her anger in the past, in fact, had resulted in more than one heated encounter between the two of them as their strange raw attraction to one another—as overpowering as a drug—kept driving them toward each other.

Dye twitched his head in irritation, surprised by how much he actually missed the confrontations, surprised that he would rather be fighting with the little temptress than to have nothing—this odd, unsettling nothing—between them. He might have thought her demotion to sergeant had sucked the life out of the proud little sprite, for all the warmth she evidenced in his presence. He *might* have thought that was the case, except for her behavior when she was off duty.

* * * * *

Surreptitiously, he sought her out at the end of the day and found her when her laughter rang across the camp. Pretending interest in something else, he turned away but slid a glance sideways to find her heading through camp with the blond sergeant at her side.

So she wasn't unhappy. She was only unhappy with him.

Upon hearing her name called out, he looked toward the source of the sound. He didn't like her name on anyone's lips but his own, he realized, and found himself grinding his teeth as the two soldiers slowed to let Brand catch up to them.

Unable to stop himself, he watched Brand saunter up to join them, stopping before her, arms crossed, knees flexing as he stood, his voice a deep murmur the king couldn't quite make out.

Taking a step to the side, he put a tent between himself and the threesome as he backed into the shadows of a tree and continued to watch as Pall broke away from the group and strode off, leaving Martigay alone with the Raith. Together, they strolled off toward the edge of camp.

Just the two of them.

Dye wanted to kill the man. With his bare hands. Instead he sent for the Captain of his Scouts and set him on some minor mission. The fact that it took a full thirty minutes for the scout to be located and report back set Dye's teeth on edge. After issuing the scout his new orders, he apologized for interrupting Brand's scheduled time off.

"Actually, you didn't interrupt anything, sir," Brand delivered with a smile that was somehow irritating. "I managed to pull off everything I wanted to and was just finishing up when your summons reached me."

* * * * *

The next day he traveled the short distance upstream to the mine, accompanied by part of his personal guard. With his main force behind him, a bulwark against the Saharat advance, and only a few hours travel between his army and his men at the mine, Dye decided ten of his guard would be enough to fend off any Saharat unwise enough to still be in the vicinity. Since the Thrallish Royal Guard traditionally went on foot, Dye chose to join them on foot and left his horse behind. Upon reaching a fairly deep river crossing, his guard felled a thick tree to span the high banks of the river.

Jumping onto the thick log behind five of his guard, Dye headed across with the rest of his guard following. Upon reaching the far bank, he automatically glanced back, his thoughts on Martigay. He found her, motionless, at the center of the log, evidently the last of his guard to follow.

"What's the problem?" he called out.

"I don't know. I...I...don't think I can move."

She appeared to be frozen in fear, staring at her feet and the water that tumbled a good eight feet below the log on which she balanced.

"Just slide your foot along. You'll be all right. If you fall into the water, we'll look for you downstream. You can swim, can't you?"

"Yes, sir. I can swim. I...I think it's the height, sir."

"Get down on your knees and crawl across."

"I c-can't, C-Commander. I'm sorry. I can't move," she shouted.

Finally moved to concern, Dye returned to the newly constructed bridge and sauntered along the log toward her. With an air of confidence meant to reassure her, he extended his hand.

Her hand shook as she inched it away from her body, toward his.

With her small hand in his, he coaxed her forward, or tried to. "Come on, Martigay. I've got you. I won't let you fall." She wouldn't move her feet. With a gently chiding curse, he yanked her into his arms. Apparently panicking, she grabbed at him, throwing him off balance.

They hit the water together, their bodies twisting and twining as they tumbled downstream. Holding his breath and wrapping his body around her, Dye took the brunt of the bumpy ride as the cold rush swept them over the river-rounded rock.

Together, they were rolling over the cobbled riverbed when the river suddenly shallowed. Digging at the rocky river bottom with knees and feet, Dye ended up on top of her and found her grinning up at him, her hair swirling beneath her in the shallows, evidently pleased with the way things had turned out—and the fact that she'd dunked the king—despite her fear of heights.

To be honest, it was worth getting wet and cold to see her smile again. Still, he wanted to wipe that wicked smile off her face, and he knew just how he wanted to do it. With his lips. Slowly, he angled his head and lowered his lips to crush hers.

In the next instant, he was getting his feet beneath him, straddling her as he stood in the thin rush of water, dragging her body through his legs as his mouth slipped on hers. Shoving Martigay behind him, he drew his steel, his eyes on the trees that guarded the riverbank.

"What is it?" she queried carefully.

Seconds later, several Saharat filtered through the trees at the river's edge. All of the men were armed with curving scimitars, while several of them carried light bows as well. Almost immediately, Dye felt her hand brush the back of his arm, just above his elbow. He shook her off, not wanting the enemy to think she might mean anything to him.

"My Lord," she whispered in a hushed tone of mortification. "I'm...I'm sorry," she stuttered, "I've placed you in danger."

"Shut up, soldier," he commanded in a low voice, "I'll handle this."

Silently, the Saharat stood motionless, apparently waiting for something or someone as Dye backed across the wide, open river, keeping the clinging girl behind him. With an arctic slash of numbing cold, the frigid rush of the river knifed at his feet and calves like a sharp sword of ice.

A horse stepped out of the trees and splashed into the shallow water, the rider finely outfitted in flowing khalat and colorful headwrap. A strong hook of a nose and the keen eyes of a predatory bird dominated the man's dark, leathery face and, as he made his way toward them, the angled rays of the sun glinted on the extravagant silver that was worked into his horse's beautiful harness.

From the back of his mount, the Saharat rider smiled down at Dye. "King Dye of Thrall, I presume? I'm the Seik Behzad of the United Saharat Clans. It's my pleasure to make your acquaintance, especially under the current circumstances...whereby I find you are my prisoner."

* * * * *

Continuing his careful retreat backward, Dye's eyes narrowed to glare at the desert aristocrat. "Why would you think I'm the king?"

"We...ah...encountered your guard upstream. Only the Ruler of Thrall travels with a guard made up entirely of Thralls. I assume you're gentleman enough to surrender in return for their lives?"

"Do I *look* like a fucking gentleman?" Dye snarled up at the man.

The man shook his head. "Not particularly. But I'm willing to reserve judgment on the matter." He squinted off into the lowering sun. "I assume the concern you're exhibiting for the woman at your back is extended to the rest of your subjects?" The Seik taunted him with a cynical smirk. "If you refuse to surrender, your guard will die. In addition, I'll do my best to kill you, too. Although..." the man leaned in his saddle to put his eyes on the woman behind the king, "I might let the girl live...for a while, at least. I find the women of your race...so attractive, so much more desirable than—"

"That's because the Saharat treat their women like shit."

The man bared his darkly stained teeth. "Women are made for a man's use. And when something's used up" the man shrugged, "you replace it."

Reflexively, Dye's fist tightened on his sword while his other hand tucked Martigay more completely behind his body.

"If you surrender, I'll guarantee your life, the lives of your men."

"The woman's one of my soldiers."

The Saharat nodded. "The lives of your soldiers, then."

"For how long?"

"For as long as your lives are useful."

"This won't stop our campaign to end your occupation of Amdahl."

Casually, the Saharat rested his forearms on the pommel of his saddle. "Perhaps not, but I imagine it will slow it down considerably, and perhaps even buy us some concessions. In the meantime, you can be my guest for this evening's meal."

* * * * *

Finding himself the Seik's reluctant guest for lastmeal, Dye forced himself to choke down a few bits of stringy meat while evaluating his surroundings. He and his host reclined on rich, thick rugs littered with embroidered pillows while trays of food were delivered and positioned on the ground between them. As he took in the interior of the long, low, desert tent, Dye's stomach cramped, wondering where they'd taken Martigay and how she fared.

Chewing on a tough bit of gristled meat, his eyes were on the Seik's two armed guards positioned either side of the tent's opening. Mentally, he calculated the distance between himself and the guards, as well as the odds and opportunity for attack. The Seik's chuckle brought his attention back to the aristocrat. As Dye regarded him coolly, the arrogant Seik stroked the jeweled hilt of the dagger tucked into the sash at his waist.

"Goat testicles," the Seik indicated, lifting a finger to point at Dye's mouth.

Dye nodded without smiling and held the Seik's amused gaze as he swallowed the mouthful after a few more grindings of his jaw. "My soldiers?" he inquired.

"They'll be joining us, momentarily," the Seik assured him. "After we've eaten."

"I'm done," Dye announced curtly, wiping his fingers on his leggings.

The Seik gave him a slight smile before he raised his hand and one of the guards at the door shouted out a command. In answer, a naked girl was shoved into the tent, through the tent's opening. Martigay. Without thinking, Dye bolted to his feet. His eyes shot daggers at the Seik. "What's this, Behzad?"

"Just a little after-dinner entertainment, King Dye." At a wave of the aristocrat's hand, Dye's Thrallish guard followed Martigay into the tent. Roped together in a line, the Thrall's wrists were secured behind their backs with several twists of rough twine.

"You guaranteed—"

"Your lives only," the Seik interrupted. "I didn't say anything about rape...or torture."

"Rape!" Dye's stomach lurched as he stared at the fabulously naked Martigay, her curves caressed by the golden light from a dozen lamps. With growing horror, he regarded the nine men of his guard. Putting two and two together—or, in this case, nine and one—he wasn't pleased with the resulting sum. "They're Thralls," he croaked out. "They'll die first, on my order."

The Saharat shrugged. "That might be entertaining."

Dye took an instant to consider the Seik's words before he shot Martigay a look of apology and regret.

"Who is this meant to punish?" he demanded abruptly. "The girl? She does this many men in a night. In fact, she's probably done *these* men in a night."

Martigay gasped and he watched her as she blinked back a stunned look of outrage. Drawing a breath, he continued. "The men? Normally, they pay her for it. They'll be glad to get a free fuck. And me? Why should I care?"

Contemplatively, the Seik lifted his brows. "You have a point, King Dye. Perhaps I'll bring in my *own* men to rape the girl."

Dye fought back the cold trickle of fear that wrapped around his spine, hoping to Hadi's Hearth his concern didn't show. "Your religion forbids rape," he pointed out with a forced sneer.

The Seik shrugged. "I'm not a particularly religious man. But...would you be more comfortable with torture?"

Affecting an expression of disinterest, Dye rolled his eyes in answer. "Bring your men in. They won't thank you for it, once they have the clap." With his challenging gaze fixed on the Seik, Dye ignored the strangled protest that came from the girl's direction.

The Seik's mouth pursed as impatience stirred in his bored features. "Do you have the clap, King Dye?"

Shaking his head in a clear expression of denial and refusal, Dye feigned horror as he stared at the man. With a signal from the Seik, two bows were trained on the king.

"Rape her mouth, if you're particular," the Seik suggested pleasantly.

Dye's face was red with anger as he ratcheted out of his chair toward her. "You'll be the death of me yet, you little slut."

Martigay bared her gritted teeth. "I hope so, My Lord."

"You *thankless* little whore." Grasping Martigay by both her upper arms, he dragged her face up to meet his as he snarled at her. "There's a blade strapped to my inner thigh," he hissed into her ear.

"I hope you don't expect me to kill myself," she hissed back.

"Of course not, you little idiot. Just get it to my hand...and I'll kill you myself."

While he yanked at his ties, she slid to her knees before him, her hands dragging down over his flanks. Pulling out his cock, he spread his legs as he fed his stiff flesh into her mouth, gasping at that first rough contact of her tongue. "Get on with it," he gritted down at her.

She took her mouth off his cock long enough to answer, "My Lord. I am on it."

The Seik's laughter caused the king to turn and glare at his captor. "Who's raping whom here, My Lord?" Behzad queried in a lazy tone of amusement.

"I can't fuck her if I'm not hard."

"I feel sorry for you," the Seik sighed. "A woman like that on her knees before you and you're not hard. You're a disappointment to all mankind, King Dye."

"The girl and I have some history between us. I can't help it if I don't find her desirable. I fear the little harlot will bite me off."

The Seik laughed, again. "That *is* the chance one takes— when one enters a woman's mouth. You might want to reconsider your alternatives," he suggested amiably.

Wrenching his cock from between her lips with an angry backward heave of his hips, Dye yanked Martigay to her feet and shoved her toward the tent's wall. "Get over there," he rasped at her. Backing toward the wall, Martigay placed herself beside one of the Seik's two men guarding the tent's opening. "Get on your knees, you little whore, and hold still."

When Martigay slid to her knees, Dye immediately braced his hands against the tightly stretched canvas at her back, pumping his hips forward as he forced his cock down her throat. Her hands were on the front of his hard thighs, fighting him away as the top of his leggings made their slow descent down his hips. Sliding one of her hands between his legs, she tasted his seed in her mouth as he started to spurt.

Then his blade was in her hand.

As her mouth filled with his release, she sucked hard, palming the steel beneath her hand and sliding it up his body. Gently, she bit on the thick flesh in her mouth—to remind him.

His hand met hers and, just afterward, the steel was ripping downward through the guts of the guard who stood beside them. With his other hand, Dye pulled the dying man's sword, turned, and flung it across the room where it stood, imbedded to the hilt, quivering in the Seik's chest.

Twisting up onto her feet, Martigay yanked Dye's dripping knife from the guard's body and threw herself at the roped line of Thralls, hacking at their bonds while Dye kicked the second guard to his knees and used the man's bow to choke the life out of him. Martigay was sawing through the last man's bonds as the king wrapped the Seik's cloak around her.

"The horses are south of us," he told the circle of Thralls, his voice hushed. "The sentries guard from without, not within. Four guards are standing outside the tent — take care of them."

Dye's hands lingered to hold her as four of his men glided silently through the tent's opening. The remainder of his guard awaited his next order but he turned Martigay and searched her eyes. "Are you all right?"

She bobbed her head. "They didn't do anything to me, other than undress me," she explained shortly.

He tipped her chin with his fist and ran his thumb over her bottom lip. "I was pretty rough with you. *Are you all right?*"

"I'm all right," she insisted as her eyes lightened. "But, just for your information," she informed him. "I don't have the clap. In addition I'm not much good for any more than five or six men a night." She squeaked as his palm made sharp contact with her bottom, then grinned up at him as he pulled her close.

"Right, then," he whispered sternly as he pushed her toward the doorway. "We're out of here."

Chapter Fourteen

"So, are you going to promote her?" Warrik was asking.

The two men, along with a few of Dye's younger lieutenants, were sharing a jar of wine in his tent. Warrik grinned at his friend. "Rumor has it that she…performed…admirably during your escape from Behzad."

Dye shot a glare at his friend at the same time that he jerked a reluctant nod of agreement. "But it was she who put us at risk in the first place." Dye hesitated. "And I'm reluctant to make a captain out of a soldier who's afraid of heights."

"Martigay? Afraid of heights?" Prithan broke in with a laugh, which ended abruptly when he took in the king's expression.

Dye's eyes narrowed on his lieutenant. "*What?*" The quiet word was a command that slashed like recently sharpened steel. "*What?*"

"Sir. It's only that…I've seen her go up the cliffs for cormorant eggs. On the coast. She…climbs…like a monkey, sir. Sergeant Palleden was beside me as we watched from below. He said she was born on the side of a cliff. Said Captain…Pawyn Martigay could skip along the walls at Veronix with her eyes closed…sir. If she wanted to…"

Dye stared at Prithan several moments before his mouth set in a hard line. "She's not afraid of heights," he stated in a low voice of revelation.

The lieutenant shook his head in answer as Warrik threw back his golden mane and laughed.

* * * * *

The king was quiet, the next dawning, as he picked at his firstmeal, a little too angry and far too edgy to eat. "Dunn," he said suddenly, to the soldier serving at his elbow.

"Sir?"

"What do you think would be the worst assignment I could give a soldier?"

"My Lord? Have I done something to anger the king?"

Dye shook his head. "Be easy, Dunn. I've no complaint with you."

"In that case, My Lord, digging privies," the old man suggested. "No," he revised his opinion, "filling in privies that have been in use for a while."

Grimly, the king nodded, then shook his head. "I don't want it to appear a punishment. Just an unpleasant assignment."

Dunn stopped to think about this. "Well, sir, speaking for myself, I don't envy the men assigned to guard the mine. Damp. Wet. Dark. Don't like tight places." The man stopped. "Well, other than the obvious exception, sir. 'Course a man my age doesn't get many exceptions, without he pays for them. And a paid woman isn't the same as…well, you know what I mean, sir."

After giving some thought to the old soldier's response, Dye sent Dunn to bring Martigay.

Pushing away from the table, he paced as he waited. He had every right to be tense, angry. Martigay's stunt had endangered the lives of his men, as well as *his* life—and her *own*!

He steeled his body to fight off a shudder of revulsion. Mithra, she'd been that close to being fucked by nine of his Thralls. His hands fisted at his sides as he paced. And after that, he'd have been forced to watch worse.

Dye shook his head. He'd not have watched. He'd have died with a bolt through his heart before he'd have stood there and watched another man touch her, let alone hurt her. And he'd have made sure he took that smug bastard, Behzad, with him.

When he heard a rustle at the doorway, he turned to face her, smoothing the hard edge of anger from his features.

"Martigay. Thank you for reporting. I'm sorry," Dye told her, forcing a serious, sympathetic mien onto his face, "but your fear of heights makes you ineligible for the promotion I'd planned for you."

At this overt lie, he watched her carefully, wanting to experience every *minute* nuance involved in her reaction. "I was going to move you back into the messengers." For an instant she appeared surprised, opened her mouth, and closed it again quickly. Dye almost laughed. If she wasn't going to help herself, and admit to her earlier deception, he damn well wasn't going to give her a hand. "However, I have another captaincy open."

"Thank you, My Lord," she said carefully, wary suspicion in every word.

Dye rolled up two sheets of parchment and put the scroll in her hand. "I'm sending you to the mines." Watching her face carefully, he found it expressionless, but thought she paled. She said nothing, however. "You're in command of a unit of fifty. There's a map in there of the mine as well as your orders admitting you—*only you*—to enter the mine. Inside the mine, there's a particularly rich vein that I want guarded."

He pointed to the scroll in her hand "I've drawn a circle around the drift. Its location must remain a secret. The men already assigned there, as well as the unit you're taking with you, mustn't know its exact whereabouts. You, alone, are to guard it and, in order to assure its secrecy, you'll have to stand sentry without lamp or light. The soldiers posted at the mine have orders to admit no one. But your orders give you permission to enter and you'll outrank everyone up there so your actions won't be questioned."

He dangled a blue ribbon in front of her.

"And my men," she stammered, "my unit of fifty. What is their assignment?"

"They're to reinforce the guard at the portal."

Nodding distractedly, she reached for the ribbon and turned.

"Martigay." When she turned back, Dye saluted her with two fingers. Apparently still rattled, she hit her forehead with her fist then turned again to make her exit.

* * * * *

Dye was still awake when his guards tried to stop the man forging into his tent. Snatching his steel from the baldric on the chair beside his cot, Dye was out of bed and crouched, steel in hand, as the intruder fought his way in past the guards. It was the girl's friend, he realized, as his guards struggled with the man just inside the tent's opening.

"Where is she?" Palleden demanded.

"Release him," the king commanded his guards. "Leave us."

Palleden straightened his rumpled sleeves as he glared at the king. "Where is she?"

"Join me in a drink, soldier?" After pulling his doeskins up his legs, Dye stepped toward the table and picked up a jar.

"Where's Captain Martigay?"

Dye glared at the man's blatant display of disrespect. "Watch yourself, soldier."

"Listen, My Lord. I don't have time to dick with you. Tell me where she is."

Dye's eyes narrowed on the man in angry disbelief.

"You can dismiss me tomorrow, flog me tomorrow, hang me tomorrow if you like. Tell me, tonight, where she is."

"She's at the mine. Guarding one of the drifts."

"Inside the *mine*?" Pall turned toward the door, then turned back. "How long has she been in there?"

Dye's stomach clenched with a sudden, sick foreboding. "The day and the night."

"Write me an order of release. *Now.*"

Folding his arms stubbornly, Dye stared at his soldier.

Pall returned his look with a cold blaze of fury. "When Martigay was a child," he started, his voice like a razor, "she woke to screams in the night. She was raised on the side of a cliff. Her family made their home in a cave. It's not unusual in the south.

"Something was in the cave, some kind of animal, tearing her family apart. She spent that long, terrifying night hunched inside the legs of a stool, staring into the blackness, waiting her turn at death while the monster fed on her family. She could hear its jaws working, rending at flesh and bone. She could feel the creature's breath, hot on the forearm that covered her eyes — just before it picked up the stool and tried to shake her out, then threw the stool across the room."

Dye's stomach tightened into a knot, recalling the long, evil scar ripping down the back of her arm. "What was it?" he asked, reaching for his linen jerkin.

"Probably a Koshiak, or something like it. She never saw it. She waited alone through the night. What she saw in the dawning was worse than anything she'd feared in the night." Wrenching the jerkin over his head, Dye yanked his vest up to follow. "She's afraid — she's terrified of the dark."

"Fuck." The king shrugged his baldric over his shoulder and dropped into his chair as he shoved his feet into his boots.

"Are you going to write that release?"

"I'll go myself," he grunted, yanking at his boots.

"You can't do that!" Pall burst out. "You'll...she'll...she'd not want you to know."

"She didn't mind my thinking she was afraid of heights."

"She what?"

"The girl pretended she was afraid of heights."

"That...then that would be different!"

"Why?"

"Because she isn't!"

Grabbing his cloak, the king strode toward the tent's opening. "You're coming with me," he said curtly.

Normally he would have ordered his horse to be harnessed by one of his men, but Dye didn't have the patience to stand idle and watch someone else fumble in the dark, struggling to do what he could easily accomplish with the aid of his Westerman eyes.

"Take the chestnut," he told Pall, thrusting a halter into his hands then reaching for his own. "How did she survive?" he asked, pulling the halter up the horse's face. "You said she was only a child when she lost her family. What did she do?"

"What any child would do," Pall answered, fumbling in the dark. "Headed downhill until she found a river and followed it downstream. Upon reaching a small farm, she offered herself and the people took her. She got lucky—they were nice people. Worked her hard, from the sounds of it, but...it could have been worse."

Reaching for a saddle, Dye shoved it at Pall before grabbing his own. "How about when she's riding at night?" he grunted.

"She's all right if she's in a crowd, with someone else," Pall answered, yanking on the girth rope. "When she's alone, she counts on her horse for company—and to warn her of any danger."

"And that's why she keeps a lamp burning all night?"

Pall shook his head. "An open flame is too dangerous in a small tent. She has a glow stone."

"She has a glow stone," Dye repeated, wonderingly.

Pall nodded. "You can imagine how long it took her to save up for that. Ten hours exposure to the sun will deliver almost that length of light come dark. It's the only way she manages to get through the night."

"I've never seen it on her belt."

Pall shook his head. "She hangs it on her saddle to recharge. The rest of the time she wears it around her neck and tucks it inside her jerkin."

"What does she do on overcast days? When the stone doesn't have a chance to recharge," he asked, stooping to release the horses' hobbles.

When Pall didn't answer right away, Dye cut a sharp glance up at his sergeant. "I sleep with her," he confessed.

With one knee on the ground, Dye's hand froze on the hobble twist as he stared at Pall.

Pall frowned down at him. "It isn't easy," he admitted in a low mutter. "I'd like to get between her legs as much as," he looked at the king and hesitated, "...the next guy. But—so far—she won't have me."

"And if she did?"

"If she gave me half a chance, I'd not waste it, My Lord."

* * * * *

Pounding into the mine's camp at a thundering gallop, Dye was dismounting before his horse had come to a complete stop. Dye hit the ground at a run. "Is the girl inside?"

"Sir?" The startled soldier standing guard at the mine's portal hurried to attention.

"Captain Martigay. Where is she?"

The soldier gave his superior a blank look and Dye grabbed the man by the shoulders as he jerked him forward. "Is Captain Martigay inside the mine?"

"My Lord! Yes, sir. She...she had orders," the man sputtered.

"Shit!

"Bring a torch," he shouted at Pall. "Martigay!" he shouted as he ducked to enter the mine's mouth.

Racing along the mine's rough, rutted track, Dye hurtled through dank, gleaming corridors hacked out of jagged rock. Knowing in exactly which drift he'd find Martigay, his night vision guided him unerringly toward the correct turning. Making a right into a narrow drift, he stopped his headlong rush, chest heaving as he searched wildly for some trace of her — then caught back a groan. He found her sitting against the wall, her knees drawn into her chest, her arms wrapped around her legs.

"Martigay," he whispered — and had her in his arms in two steps. She screamed just before she turned to dead weight in his arms. She'd fainted. Looking down on her, he watched her arms uncurl from her chest to droop toward the floor as her knotted hands loosened. He heard a small clatter and watched a smooth, round stone roll a few inches and rock to a stop. Staring down at the stone, he winced with regret.

It was her glow stone. As dull and lifeless as the woman he clutched in his arms. Stooping carefully, he reached for the stone and wrapped it up in the center of his palm.

* * * * *

Upon returning to his camp at the river, Dye threw his mount's reins to one of his men. With the unconscious girl still in his arms, he slid carefully from his horse and carried her into his tent where he sat with her, the fingers of one hand inside her jerkin, beneath her chemise, tucked into her warm cleavage where he could feel the reassuring pulse of her heart. When Pall was announced, he looked up at the young sergeant. "I've broken down her mount and raised her tent," Pall told him.

Dye nodded as his arms curled to hold her possessively.

"She'd not want you to know…about this," Pall persisted.

"She shouldn't be left alone," Dye informed him.

"I wasn't going to leave her alone," Pall answered in challenge.

The two men stared at each other, neither giving ground. "She won't know one man from another in the dark," Dye finally said, making his intention clear as he stood with the girl in his arms, brushing past his sergeant on the way across the tent. "I'll be out of her tent at first dawning. Her glow stone's on the table. Make sure it gets recharged," he ordered.

Chapter Fifteen

The king's guards exchanged grins as they watched their commander stoop to enter Martigay's tent.

Although it was black inside her shelter, Dye's night vision allowed him to see Martigay as plainly as if it were midday. Carefully, he eased the limp girl out of her jerkin and lowered her onto her mat. When he unlaced her leggings and drew them down her legs, her shorts were dragged away along with the doeskins. Pleased with this result, as well as the view, he didn't bother to rectify the situation.

For a long time he just watched her. She was art for the eyes, the sensuous lines of her perfect form rounding over her naked hips on their way to her thighs, curling into her knees and sweeping down to her ankles. Slowly, his eyes followed the gentle curves along the inside of her legs back up to where they merged, then split at the delta of her sex, darkened with the rich, red velvet curling in her groin.

Only her thin cotton chemise covered her, and nothing else. Painfully threadbare, the worn fabric that strained to cover her nipples was almost transparent. Laced down the front, it was probably originally closed with a ribbon but now a tattered bit of string was all that kept it together over her full, round breasts.

Stretching out carefully, Dye lay down beside her.

Despite the fact that he moved carefully, he must have roused her, because she reached for him as soon as he was settled. She woke suddenly, calling for Pall and clutching at his leather vest as she pulled herself into his arms.

Automatically, every muscle in his body tightened—one muscle in particular—as his hand hovered uncertainly in the air above her hip. When he let it fall, his palm followed the rounded flesh over her hip to curve and hold her bottom. Years of habit, as well as strong male instinct worked on him to pull her lower body tightly against his. He thought he would be content then, with her body close to his.

He wasn't.

His hand kept moving and he couldn't stop himself to save his place at Hadi's Hearth, let alone his principles. His fingers spread and traveled over her bottom, up into the small of her back, drawing her closer, returning to her bottom, pulling her thigh toward him.

Martigay roused slowly to the pleasant sensation of a man's fingers in her crease then on her thigh, dragging her leg to drape over his hip.

"Pall?" she murmured. The hand on her thigh hesitated only an instant before it continued. Stroking gently, but insistently, the hand pulled her up into the man's hard, heated advance. Opening her eyes, she frowned into the darkness, but could see nothing of the man beside her. The darkness made her shudder and he pulled her closer. "Th...thanks for g-getting me out of that m-mine," she stammered as she shivered. "I was...it was—"

"Shhh," he breathed against her ear.

"Bastard," she gritted out. The hand on her leg stopped. "The king," she clarified. "Effing, pronking bastard."

All at once, she was on her back as his upper body covered hers. "I'm sorry," he whispered and his lips covered her mouth.

Suddenly desperate to feel her naked breasts beneath his palms, Dye broke away from her lips as his fingers tangled with the ties that drew her thin chemise tight across her nipples. She murmured a protest as she pushed away from him but the action did nothing to reduce his lust or halt his advance. Tugging at the ties, he got several fingers through the laces to stroke over the round, warm curve of her breast. When his rough thumb grazed her nipple, he held his breath as her eyes opened, searching the darkness.

"No," she murmured uncertainly. "No, Pall."

Watching her face, Dye pushed his hand further into the chemise, forcing the opening to widen until the pale peach of her nipple was partly exposed at the edge of the chemise, beneath the loosely crossed ties. His hand rounded the far side of her breast and he lifted the plump weight in his palm as the whole of her nipple was bared in the loosened opening of her chemise.

Her eyes were wide and fixed on a point just below his as she frowned in the darkness. "No," she breathed, her hands against his chest.

Sliding his hand back over the smooth skin beneath her chemise, he knotted his fingers in her ties. One yank and the strings were out. Pulling his body away from her, his hand shook as he laid the chemise open, exposing her beautiful breasts. Warm peach nipples were centered on the full, heavy breasts that slipped to the sides of her chest.

Heart racketing, dick pounding, he watched her sleepy attempt to pull the chemise closed again. His hands tangled briefly with hers as he pushed them aside to scrape his palm over one of her nipples. Under his persistent, teasing touch, her nipples tightened into knots that caught at his fingers and, slowly, he lowered his mouth to the circle of petal-peach.

Her hands tugged at his hair as his lips tugged the nipple to a rough point, and when she pulled his hair beyond the point of comfort, he took hold of her wrists and pinned her arms wide while he dipped his head and licked each of her nipples into hard, glistening peaks.

Sucking areola and nipple suddenly into his mouth, he felt her feeble struggles cease beneath him as her body stiffened and her back arched to push her breasts up into his mouth. With a small grin of satisfaction, he raised his eyes to her face, brushing her wet nipples with his stubbled chin. Her breath caught in her throat and her eyes closed as she gave—and he accepted—her total surrender.

Her beautifully formed body was smooth and naked under his weight and, immediately upon taking her lips, he felt himself losing control. Like a man drowning in the midst of floating wreckage, he clung to the small red scrap of her lips, glad she'd surrendered because nothing short of a crowbar was going to stop him now. Restlessly he positioned and repositioned his mouth over the soft, yielding lips that accepted — without reservation — his ravaging onslaught, his tongue thrusting and taking and tasting the warm interior of her mouth as his lips quested for some sort of satisfaction in hers, knowing damn well the answer wasn't in her mouth — and couldn't be reached with his tongue.

Pulling her back onto her side, he grasped her thigh firmly and dragged it high on his waist, tucking her ankle behind his back. Sweeping his hand back down her thigh to her bottom, he brushed his open hand across her cheeks, where they stretched apart. Several times he repeated the action, reveling in the humid warmth beneath his palm before dropping his fingers into the damp heat at the base of her open cheeks. Gently, he tugged on a round cheek as he let his fingers brush into the folds tucked into her damp sex.

As Martigay's breathing changed, the small variation of sound set his heart on edge and his cock expanded inside his doeskin leggings. Carefully, meticulously, he explored every nook and cranny of the fragile ruts and folds tucked inside her puffy labia. As he played his fingertips over her damp, full sex, he found her clit and dabbed it with his little finger while the rest of his fingers slid down to rest at her opening.

Like a young fawn caught in the hunter's target — too stunned to run — she stilled.

Tucking his chin into his chest, Dye gazed down on her face to find her wide-eyed and waiting for his fingers' further incursion. Gently, he scraped his little finger over her clitoris while he let the tips of his three remaining fingers press into her opening. Her breath caught in her throat and her knee moved higher on his body, separating her cheeks further, opening her sex wider to allow him greater access. At the same time, a flood of liquid seeped around the fingers set inside her vulva. Her lips parted in a whispered moan and his fingers slipped on the slick, wet surface of her sex as he continued to play with her clit at the same time that he pumped his fingertips into her flooding vagina.

Now small cries spilled from her parted lips and her body shifted, restless beneath his hand, her knee climbing further up his side, almost into his armpit. Dragging his hand out of her pussy, he loosened his ties with one hand and freed his cock as he rolled her onto her back.

With a knee between her legs, he made room for himself, got between her yielding thighs and positioned his blunt tip at her entrance. Expecting little resistance, he pushed into her, anticipating a slick, easy advance.

But in the next instant, he was gritting his teeth to contain his release. Dye heard Martigay's sharp gasp as her body fought his entry, her vulva choking on the thick head of his cock. Reining in his increasingly heated male instinct, he gave her a moment, unwilling to give any ground or retreat in any manner, then inched into her. Again her cunt cinched tightly around his cock head and again he waited for her body to adjust to his presence before he gave her another careful inch. Sweat dampened his brow as Dye stared down into her face to find an uncomfortable little frown between her wide eyes. Suddenly he was swept with an unanticipated rush of tenderness.

Martigay. She had to be the biggest little fake he'd ever stumbled across in his lifetime. Aye, he had a lot going for him between his legs. But the woman talked like she had men for breakfast, lunch and dinner and ate them whole without swallowing.

But this little fake hadn't had a man in quite a while. And that was no lie. Lowering his lips until they touched her forehead, he pressed them into her rumpled little frown. "Martigay," he whispered.

He wanted to reassure her, somehow. Let her know that she was doing all right, that there was no hurry. That he'd wait for her and give her the time along with anything else she needed to receive him—make room for him—inside her. That he'd make it right for her and not leave her behind. That she was safe in his hands. But all he could mange to choke out was, "Easy, Martigay."

Slowly, he continued his advance in installments, coaxing her legs up beside his body in order to complete his entry and immerse himself to the hilt inside her warm slit. Finally he was there, fully extended, wrapped up and soaking in her warm depths, his cock head nudging the back of her sheath as her vagina held the length of his shaft tightly.

Experimentally, he pulled a few inches and gave them back.

Her body was stiff beneath his, as though still trying to contend with so much all at once.

Mesmerized—the normally savage edge of his passion subdued in wonder—he watched her face as he coaxed her body forward with the brush of his fingers, the caress of his palm. With curving fingers, he stroked her breast, circled her nipple languorously with one rough fingertip, licked his fingers and pulled on the tiny peach peak then blew on it until it was dry and stiff and achingly tight. Slowly, he smoothed his hand down over her waist, past her hip to caress her bottom, lifting it gently, rhythmically to meet his groin, starting her into the action she'd soon take and make her own.

With his hand wrapping one of the round firm cheeks of her bottom, he put a kiss on her lips. And, though the kiss started gently, it rapidly became ravenous. Finally succumbing to the passionate need that rode him with a vengeance, his mouth ate into hers, his tongue intruding roughly between her lips as, with a hand on her bottom, he pulled her body up to meet his grinding hips.

The action between her legs that had started shallow and smooth had, by now, accelerated into a body-jarring, brutal, free-for-all with her soft, feminine cunt on the receiving end of his hard male barrage. Somehow, the corded muscles of his upper arm found their way under one of her thighs, pressing her leg high, opening her sex for his complete penetration.

She cried out—a small, helpless sound of whispered need and his heart wrenched as he slowed to listen. Her breath caught in her throat several times and he knew she was close. When he returned his lips to hers, she whimpered, then clutched, and he realized she was coming, her vagina tightening to hug the length of his cock.

"Ah, Mithra, Martigay," he whispered, and held hard inside her as he came.

"Oh. My. Lord. Mithra," Martigay gasped out in fragments torn from a mouth open in surprised bliss and Dye buried his mouth in her neck to muffle his roar of pleasure as his release shot through his shaft to fill her with his jetted stream of cum and her cunt closed to hold his cock.

When her body was finished wringing out his cock, he rolled to lie beside her, collecting her in one arm as she pressed up against him. She purred inside his arm—a high, soft note—a sound of pure female contentment. Sighed and purred again as she snuggled into him as closely as she could.

Dye's arm tightened around her to pull her closer.

He felt like he couldn't fucking breathe. Tight and tense, as though one good deep breath would shatter him. There was a hard lump stretching his throat that was impossible to swallow around, and it felt as though a bear trap had clamped on his heart, while at the same time there was a tight knot in his stomach.

He'd wanted this fuck ever since he'd laid eyes on the little wildcat. Dreamed of it. Imagined her spreading her legs wide as he came to her and rose over her, and drove into her, mounting her with one hard, overpowering push as she canted her hips to meet and receive his every thrust. Martigay—taking everything he could give and demanding more with her sexy gutter mouth. Screaming into orgasm as her nails bit into his ass and she thrashed under his body, her legs opening impossibly wide at the last instant to take him hard at the back of her cunt—loving it—screaming to be fucked forever.

But the wicked, wanton Martigay was a little lady on the mat.

He thought his heart would blow into pieces.

Mithra!

It was a mistake to lay the girl, he thought, lying awake with only his guilty conscience for company, Martigay curled and asleep at his side. It had been a mistake. Forcing a breath deep into his lungs, he gazed down on the woman beside him. It had been a mistake, all right. A mistake he'd not change for anything in the world.

With Martigay warm at his side, Dye watched the night gradually give way to gray dawn, bright in his Westerman eyes. Inwardly, he sighed. With the dawn, there were a thousand tasks that must be attended. And he'd best be out of her tent before the whole army was up to see him—to know where he'd spent the night.

Quietly, he slipped from beside her, yanking his ties closed as he backed out of her tent. When he reached his own pavilion, he motioned one of his guards to follow him inside.

"Send Captain Martigay to me the first you see her," he told the man.

Throwing himself into a chair, Dye went to work, temporarily setting aside the fact that he'd soon have to face the girl, and that he had a lot of explaining ahead of him.

Chapter Sixteen

A rustle of sound caused the king to raise his eyes. Just inside the tent's opening, stood Martigay. For two instants, he stared at her before he realized he wasn't breathing. *Andarta!* The woman was breathtaking if nothing else. He stood without thinking.

Her face was lit with a warm glow, her cheeks flushed pink, eyes filled with a surreal, smoky light. Abstractly, she frowned at him, her fingers twisting the braid in her hair, her expression troubled.

"Do you believe in love at first sight, My Lord?" she put to him, out of the blue.

Slowly, he shook his head.

She nodded. "Neither do I." She took a few uncertain steps forward and lowered herself into a chair before his table. "We got off to a rocky start."

He nodded as he slowly sank back into his chair.

"And I've known him for years."

Him!

"I would never have guessed I could feel this way about him," she said quietly. "I would never have guessed I could feel this way about *any* man, let alone Pall."

"*Pall!*"

"To think of all the times I pushed him away." Martigay stopped there, as she seemed to search for something in the man seated before her—then flicked her head as if to toss aside some complicated riddle. "I didn't know what I was turning down! But now…after last night—" she shivered and her eyes lost their focus. "But now—" She stood suddenly, heading toward the exit, apparently having forgotten that the *king* had sent for *her*. "I wonder what he's doing just now."

"If you find him, send him here," he put in swiftly.

She turned back with a slow expression of surprise. "Okay," she said, "but it might take me…oh…twenty minutes or so to find him."

"If it takes you more than five, you're a pawyn again, Martigay."

She looked bemused. "It's going to be hard to pull off a wedding in five minutes, My Lord."

"Wedding!" he sputtered. "You can't wed a man based on one night of—"

"—the best sex I've ever had in my life."

"One night of—" he continued, then stopped. "Was it?"

"Was it what?"

"What you said. The best sex."

"I don't joke about things like that," she said, nodding seriously. "His timing, his delivery was…perfect. If I didn't know otherwise, I'd think I'd lain with a god last night. One of the younger ones," she added hastily. "Thor, perhaps. Although it wasn't just sex," she added as an afterthought.

Leaning back in his chair, he arched an eyebrow in her direction.

"You'd not understand."

"Try me."

"It was…like we were made for each other. As though we came together and the point at which we came together was the point at which everything started and ended, and was the point at which everything mattered." She shrugged with an apologetic little grin. "I told you that you'd not understand."

"Nay," he admitted, his eyes never leaving her face. "I'd not understand. Unless…it was like the ultimate fuck. The fuck you want to last forever, the fuck you want to never end, the fuck you want to hold onto for all time, knowing you'd do whatever it would take to hold onto it. Finally losing hold, letting go in arrival, and finding the losing even better than the holding. Opening your eyes at the end of orgasm and hardening again, just thinking of the perfect coming.

"And afterward, telling yourself—arguing with yourself— that it could be just as good, just the same, with the next woman. Knowing in the same instant that you're wrong, that you're kidding yourself at worst and lying to yourself at best. Knowing that it will never be the same again. Knowing, *knowing*, that your life was going to be useless without the next one. The next fuck. With the same woman. For as long as you can possibly keep her." His eyes cut a challenge at hers. "But I'd not understand."

She stared at him gape-mouthed for two instants before her jaw snapped closed. And for those two instants, he feared he'd offended her. But she smiled slowly. "I think that's the most romantic thing I've ever heard out of a man. I've underestimated you, Dye," she said, "you *do* take sex seriously."

"But," she said, with a sigh. "You should have taken me up on my offer when you had the chance, My Lord." Turning, she moved toward the exit again. "Because, as of today, I'm no longer available."

"Martigay!"

Once more, she turned to face him.

"As disappointing as that news is, let me remind you that *I* sent for *you* and, lest you've forgotten, *I'm* your commanding officer."

She blinked at him in recognition as the dreamy haze in her eyes dissipated.

He motioned toward the chair before his table. "Take a seat."

Moving across the room, Martigay obediently slipped into the chair as Dye considered her face for several moments, planning his approach. She looked defensive.

"We need to talk," he started, "about last night. As well as your next assignment."

She gave him a curt nod, as she fingered her braid. "I imagine you'll be wanting this ribbon back."

"No. No," he answered swiftly. "Let's leave that for now. But about last night."

"Did Pall tell you? About the cave?"

"Yes, but—"

"He shouldn't have said anything."

"I'm glad he did," he said gently.

But she took it the wrong way. "I'll just bet you are," she returned in a flat voice.

She might as well have smacked him across the face. A long silence separated them before he stood and turned his back to her. Wrong approach, he decided, forcing himself to be patient. Evidently, she assumed he would use this information against her, perhaps to demote her once more.

"*Captain Martigay,*" he spoke the words with great emphasis. "Let me tell you about your next assignment. I'd like you to take over supply."

"But you said there weren't any positions…"

"Let me speak, Captain!" Turning to face her, he continued in a very businesslike manner. "I'd like you to take over supply. Several wagons are arriving this morning and I need someone I can trust in charge of management and distribution. There have been a few complaints from Destri's unit and I'd like someone to oversee the distribution of his allotment, in particular. Make sure that everything is fair. Are you comfortable doing that?"

"Sir?"

"Do you want the job?"

"Yes, sir!"

"You'll have to put off your wedding plans," he pointed out with a straight face, "for today, anyway."

She grinned and nodded.

"Thank you, Captain. Please find Sergeant Palleden and send him to me, then ask Lieutenant Greegor to pull out fifty men for you."

"Will I be under Greegor's command?"

He shook his head. "You'll report directly to me. If you'll report here at the end of the day, I'll help you get started on the next requisition. In addition, we still have some unfinished business to discuss."

"Sir?"

"It would be better discussed later, Martigay. After you've had a day to adjust to your new duties. You're dismissed."

Her duties would delay any plans she had for wedding—at least for today—he decided wryly, standing at his tent's opening and watching Martigay's sexy saunter through camp.

Grinding his teeth in the next instant, he watched her with Palleden and almost launched himself across camp when he saw her hand linger to caress the sergeant's thigh. He saw Palleden's surprised reaction. She told him something—spoke to him—and the blond's eyes traveled across camp to connect with the king's. With a brisk turn, the sergeant made his way toward his commander.

Moments later Pall stood within the king's tent.

"She thinks it was you with her last night," Dye muttered in a low, rough-edged voice.

"I gathered that!"

"Why didn't you set her straight?"

"Why didn't you?" Pall shot back.

"I tried to!"

Dye glared at the young sergeant before he shook his head. "If I'm close enough to tell her, she'll be close enough to kill me. I don't want to be anywhere *near* her when she finds out. She's going to be mad." His expression was wry as he fell into his chair. "She said the *two of you* got off to a rocky start."

Pall nodded, dropping into the chair before the king's table. Reaching to his waist, he pulled three nutshells from a pouch tied to his belt and placed them on the table. Holding a dried pea between his thumb and forefinger, he showed it to the king then placed it carefully beneath one of the shells. Slowly, he began to move the shells on the table's smooth surface. As he wove the shells in and out, around each other, at increasing velocity, he spoke to the king.

"This little trick was always good for a few drinks," he explained just before his hands stopped. "Where's the pea?" he asked the king.

Dye's lips drew together in shrewd consideration. "In your hand," he answered.

Pall nodded. "You've a keen eye, My Lord. So does the girl. She accused me of cheating in a tavern full of…losers." Pall shrugged. "I had my honor to defend…as well as my life," he muttered. "I threw my ale in her face."

The king blinked as Pall nodded wryly. "What did she do?"

"'You'll pay for that', she told me. Then she picked up my shells and beat me at my own game, though her sleight-of-hand was atrocious. Won back all the money I'd…" Pall coughed, "won. And bought the tavern a round, thereby saving my ass."

"The imp." The king shook his head in admiring wonder. "After she'd put your ass to risk, in the first place."

"Aye," Pall laughed. "And the thing of it is…the most *amazing* thing of it is…I don't know how she did it. I still don't know!"

The king's eyes were keen on his soldier as the sergeant pushed back his chair and stood. He raised his chin to the young officer. "She wants to wed you."

Pall grinned just before he swaggered toward the door then turned back to face the king. "Write her a note and don your armor, My Lord. That would be my suggestion. And do it soon. Because—I'm warning you, sir—if she asks me to wed her, I'm not turning her down."

* * * * *

A meeting with Greegor and the Khallic Princes kept Dye busy for most of the afternoon and, for the time being, he put aside the confession that would have to be made at the end of the day.

After catching up on correspondence, he laid out a few examples of earlier requisitions and ate lastmeal at his table, glancing at the tent's opening and wondering about Martigay while he formulated his next approach…to the truth. When he'd finished his meal, he changed clothing and pulled a comb through his hair, still wondering where Martigay was, before finally heading toward the tent's exit—where he was almost bowled over by one of his guards rushing in with an announcement.

"My Lord. It's two of your captains," the man wheezed out in an apprehensive rush of words.

With a dread feeling of premonition, the king hurried after his guard.

Elbowing his way through the rough circle of onlookers, Dye found his two captains scuffling in the dust. From the sounds of things, the man on top appeared to be choking back laughter. The woman beneath him, however, was not.

Martigay.

Destri rolled on top of her, straddling her on his knees, leaning forward to pin her wrists to the ground, laughing outright as he did so. In a scorching burst of fury that blindsided him, he had Captain Destri by the collar. "Get off her!" he snarled in a violent hiss of fury.

The man left the ground on his way to land four feet distant. Immediately, the two combatants scrambled to their feet and Dye watched Martigay launch herself at Destri again. Hooking her above the elbows from behind, Dye dragged her off Destri. Still she kicked and struggled to free herself and resume the conflict. Shoving her behind him, Dye spread a hand in the middle of her chest to restrain her. "Captain Martigay! Get a grip, soldier!"

Chest heaving, the girl panted beneath his hand. Dye looked to Destri then back at her. "What is this about?"

There were several instants of hard-bitten silence. "It's private," she finally gritted out, her eyes still looking daggers at Destri while Destri returned his cool amusement.

"Destri?"

The man offered nothing but a keen, taunting smile.

"How private could it be!?" Dye demanded as he glared around the circle of men who ringed the clearing. When he caught Dunn's eye, he lifted his chin at the man, and the old soldier cleared his throat as his eyes shuttered, looking for a way out. "Dunn!"

"Sir. Captain Destri called Martigay…" Dunn eyed Destri uncomfortably, "the 'King's little captain'."

An instant's silence followed, as the king shook his head—and shook it again in frustration. "Is that it? Is that all?"

"Sir. Captain Destri intimated that Captain Martigay's rank might be due to the fact that she's…bedding the king."

At this, Dye had to hold Martigay back as she attempted to make a new break for Destri. "Destri?" the king inquired coldly.

Though a sheen of nervous perspiration dampened his upper lip, Destri responded with a sneer of contempt. That look of scorn was for the girl, Dye realized, wanting to kill Destri before the man could take another breath, knowing this was nobody's fault but his.

"Destri!"

"I said nothing that wasn't true. The girl was offended that I would bring up the small matter that she was…that you and her were—everyone knows it," he argued. "More than one man saw you enter her tent last night."

Dye felt her stiffen beneath his outstretched hand. *Everyone but Martigay*, he thought, a sick knot cramping his stomach. "So you accused the captain of fucking her way to success.

"You owe Captain Martigay an apology," he said in a voice like scraping steel. "Her advancement in my army has been a result of her performance *in the field. Not* in my bed." He didn't look at her as she elbowed her way out of his hold. "*Apologize!*"

Destri's eyes flicked angrily. "I apologize, Captain Martigay," he delivered, but only grudgingly.

"You're dismissed," the king hissed, then more loudly, "all of you."

Every muscle bunched for assault, he turned to face her. For a long time she stood staring off into the distance, her fingers twisting at the bottom of the braid that held her ribbon of rank. Finally she undid the knot, pulled out the ribbon, and dropped it on the ground.

"Martigay. Where are you going?" He trailed her to her tent, along with the two Thralls shadowing him. "Where are you going?" he repeated as she pulled an axe from her kit and used it to hook her tent pegs out of the ground. Violently, she yanked at each peg as he watched. He turned on his guards. "Leave us!" he rasped. Then, "Get back or lose your lives." His Thralls moved off a few paces as, turning back to her, he wiped his damp palms on his thighs. "Martigay," he said softly, "was it so bad?"

She nodded once, sharply, before she stopped and looked up to finally meet his eyes. "I thought it was Pall." Folding the tent on the ground, she began to roll it. "You must have known that."

"I didn't think you'd be adverse to the idea. You've certainly shown enough interest…in me…in the past."

"That was before I spent thirty-odd hours in that *fucking* mine, courtesy of My Lord, the King," she scraped out. "That sort of thing can put a real damper on a girl's enthusiasm.

"And *if* I were bedding the king," she continued with accelerating fury, "I'd be a great deal more discreet about it. For *that* reason" she nodded back toward the clearing where the fight had taken place, "for starters!

"Everyone knew," she muttered to herself in tight, high tones. "Everyone but me. And I," she exploded, "tried to deny it all. Deny I was bedding the king when everyone knew I was. You've made me look like a liar at Mithra's very *fucking* best, and a complete *idiot* at worst."

"I only came to your tent in case you woke in the darkness," he said quietly, glancing behind him as he did so. "I wasn't going to touch you." Retreating a few steps, he dropped to sit on a rock. "I wasn't going to touch you," he repeated, "but I...couldn't keep my hands off you. You have a body...that would drive a saint to rape."

"That doesn't excuse *you*! You may be a king, but you fall *well* short of being a saint." Her voice grated at him as she fought to regain some semblance of self-control. "You took advantage of me at a moment of weakness," she said, without looking at him. "You took me while I still shivered with fear. You took me *knowing* I thought you were Pall, and without bothering to set me straight before you entered me. You took me knowing I was angry *at you* for putting me in the mine. Knowing I would have refused you.

"Then! *Then!*" she screeched. "You let me sit in your tent and make an ass of myself going on about how wonderful you were on the mat! *Me*—thinking I was talking about Pall. You sat there and let me feed your insufferable, undeserving ego." Her voice cracked a bit. "You took me at a moment of weakness," she repeated, her voice crumpling completely.

He watched her tie her tent in a roll, feeling breathless, feeling sick, knowing she was right and had a right to be angry with him. Knowing that in a few minutes she'd be on her horse and gone.

"I took you at a moment of weakness," he admitted to her—to himself. "I'm not going to let you go." The words hung in the air, strangely alone, surprising him as much as they probably surprised her.

She stared at him, apparently as stunned by the statement as he was. "You're not going to stop me!" she asserted.

He said nothing as she replaced the axe in her kit then threw tent and kit toward her pony. Turning away from him, she reached for her saddle.

Behind her, Martigay heard him start away from her camp, followed by his voice as he commanded his guards. "Bring Captain Martigay to my tent, immediately." Her head came up in anger as he turned to catch her eye. "Use whatever means necessary to restrain her," he told his men without looking at them. "But see to it that she's not harmed."

Chapter Seventeen

Dye kicked back in his chair as his first guard broke into the tent. The second followed. Trussed hand and foot, the girl was inelegantly slung over the shoulder of the second Thrall. "Sir," the first man wheezed, "where would you have her?"

With a flick of his wrist, Dye indicated the thick pole supporting the tent's roof. With one knee bent and his foot against the table's leg, he pushed himself back to rock on the chair's back legs.

Only after a great deal of scuffling, the two guards managed to wrestle Martigay to the pole, get her hands untied and retied again behind her. Saluting their captain, the Thralls strode from the tent.

Sliding her back up the pole, Martigay yanked silently at her bonds. From across the tent, Dye watched her struggle.

Finally, she glared at him, her lips set in a wordless straight line.

Although darkness was only just closing in, Dye's attendant had lit several lamps to fill the tent with a warm, flickering glow. For several moments, he watched her standing in the warm wash of light as his eyes swept her body and his gaze slowed to linger at those places that most held his interest.

With a shove, his chair scraped backward. He moved to stand before her and stopped when a scant foot separated their bodies. Pulling off his vest, he threw it behind him on the desk. Crossing his arms, he reached for the bottom of his linen jerkin and ripped it over his head. "What are you doing?" she gritted out at him.

Without answering, he tugged at his ties and Martigay watched the gap widen beneath the loosely crossing strings, the thick ridge of his cock encouraging the gap to part. "I don't want clothing to be an issue," he explained brusquely.

His hand was under her jerkin and on her waist before she realized it. She gasped at the strong, rough touch of hard, male fingers. She opened her mouth to complain but only gasped again when his other hand cupped her breast, his body came up hard against hers, and his lips took the words right out of her mouth.

She was still trying to get a breath when he groaned into her mouth, the sound a wordless male demand for more, while at the same time a stated admission of vulnerability, aching with a need that rocked her right to her foundation. Again she was robbed of breath as her head tilted back beneath his and his mouth was forced restlessly against hers, the edge of a tooth snagging her upper lip and bruising it against her own teeth.

Against her own will, her rebel body responded with a flash flood of erotic warmth that seeped through her system and spilled into her vagina to dampen her pussy. Body straining, she began to reach for everything he put in her mouth with a hungry voracity that only encouraged his ruthless advance and accelerated the intensity of his actions.

He got his hands beneath her jerkin and fought upward in the tight space inside her chemise to find her breasts, and feel the naked, damp skin against his rough palms. Finding his access restricted, he pulled his hands out to fumble impatiently at the ties across her breasts at the same time that she sobbed into his mouth. "Dye," she rasped in a whisper, as his lips smeared into hers. "Mithra, Dye."

With the ties only just unknotted, the jerkin only just opened, his fingers tried to find a way to her breasts again. Desperate for the feel of her, he forced his hand down into the top of her chemise. When the frail cotton shredded, he broke away from her lips to watch his hand round her breast, his thumb catch at her tight nipple. Her head arched back and her back bowed to feed her breast into his hand, into his rough touch as his finger joined his thumb to tug at the rumpled peach flesh caught in the trembling pinch of his grip.

Her voice caught back a strangled cry — a cry for more — and he lowered his head to her breast, lifting its full weight with his hand to meet his mouth. Mouth open, he scraped his teeth over the roughly textured surface of her nipple then sucked in as much breast as would fit in his mouth — hard. When he let her go, he put a gentle sucking kiss on her upright nipple. Her cry was a helpless, wanton demand for more.

"Hadi's Saints." His curse was a harsh whisper as he straightened. Automatically, his groin was crushing into hers, as his hips rocked to slide the ridge of his cock against her lower body. "Mithra," he gasped. "Martigay, I've got to get these leggings off you."

Her hips were reaching for him as he pulled at her ties and rucked the doeskins down past her sex. Pressed up against her, he pushed a hand between her legs to dip his fingers into her pussy. Together they moaned as his fingers moved through the thick, wet folds.

"Mithra Fucking Andarta On Her Knees," he cursed, his lips hot against hers as he spoke into her mouth. "Don't tell me you don't want me, girl. You're creaming into my hand. Your sweet little piece is cock-hungry and begging for a man."

With the bud of her clitoris trapped between his fingers, he watched her face as he scissored his fingers in rhythm to the pulse filling his hand.

"Dye," she whimpered with every ragged intake of breath, the sound a whispered litany of desire.

Swiftly, he fell to his knees and kissed the top of her pussy, brushing his lips against the thick, warm fullness of her labia, working his lips into her soft, full sex, using the tip of his tongue to part her cleft. Exploring her hidden folds with his tongue, he pushed into the flesh as it gave around his entry and felt her body tremble as he shot his tongue as deeply into her as he could with her legs tied together.

"No!" she cried suddenly.

Roughly, he dragged his flattened tongue up inside the entire line of her sex. "Don't tell me to stop," he growled. "You're streaming into my mouth, girl. You want this as badly as I do."

"No. Not yet." Martigay struggled to reclaim her lower body and, wrenching her hips, tried to pull her pussy away from his face. Relentlessly, he followed, his mouth open and sucking at her felted lips. "No. Dye. Not yet. I want you inside."

She groaned as his tongue moved in and out more rapidly, more ruthlessly, stabbing roughly through the front of her cleft, his tongue pushing and pulling her clitoris toward climax.

Her body shuddered beneath his mouth and her skin was damp where he held her sweating hips. Stopping to gaze up the length of her straining body, Dye ran a hand between her legs to find the inside of her thighs running with the result of her lust. With his hand, he followed the stream of moisture up to her opening, testing the waters carefully as they seeped from her vulva in preparation for his penetration. Leaning forward, he slid his tongue into her again, slowly, at the same time his thumb pressed to take her vagina and the grip of his forefinger moved up into her crease to cover the tight crimp of her ass.

"Untie me," she moaned. "Mithra and Donar Both. Untie my legs, Dye." Holding her sex firmly in his grip, he ignored her as he played his tongue through her folds again. "Don't make me come like this."

He pulled his head back far enough to look up at her. "You don't want to come like this? How do you want to come, Martigay?"

"With you. With you inside me."

"With my cock inside you?"

Helplessly, she nodded.

"With your legs spread, wide and open, while I fuck you?"

"Dye, please."

"All right," rasped roughly. "Show me, sweetheart. Open your legs for me."

Pulling his knife from the sheath on his hip, he slid the blade through the rope at her ankles and got rid of her leggings and shorts. Pushing her legs open, he hesitated long enough to put a long, sucking kiss on her puffy little clit. As he suckled, his hand rubbed restlessly over his erection, sweeping down to smooth over his testes and up his length again. Spreading his knees, he pulled his cock out of his leggings and pumped himself slowly in rhythm to the tongue working in Martigay's swollen sex. Her legs relaxed to widen and her hips rocked as she fed her warm, wet pussy into his mouth. Barely moving his mouth, he let her work herself against his face. Until she stopped.

"Look at you," he breathed, "your pussy open—your cunt wet and hot and hungry." He rose before her. "You're ready for my cock and the rest of the fuck. Aren't you?" he whispered, nipping the delicate shell of her ear between his teeth. With a hand underneath her thigh, he pulled her leg high as he positioned the wide head of his dick at the mouth of her opening. Then, in one long, even thrust, he entered the throat of her sex, forcing his cock head to the back of her sheath while the length of her slim channel struggled to accommodate his width.

Relinquishing his grip on her leg to hold her head in both hands, he forced her mouth to accept his tongue's intrusion while giving her vagina a scant moment to acclimate to his presence. Then his hands slid down to her hips and he held her on his cock while he crushed into her—one unforgiving thrust at a time, watching her face as she approached arrival, then watching their bodies where they were joined—where he rode into her.

Her legs stole upward and he helped her get them to his waist where they wrapped to lock around his body as he continued to pound into her constricting channel, hammering his way to cock-busting arrival, knowing he was about one bang away from orgasm and waiting for her sign before taking his own release.

Mithra Fucking Andarta, she was something when she came. Like a flame touched to liquid fire, spilling hot and unquenchable around his dick. In a helpless fit of ecstasy, wild and out of control, she thrashed beneath the weight of his body shoving her into the pole. He felt the pressure tighten in his scrotum, the long flash of pleasure that claimed his lower body, then he was shooting into her in a long, hot, steady stream of burning cum.

"Mithra," he groaned at the end of his arrival, leaning against her damp, used body, skimming his lips across her forehead to press them into her temple. "Mithra!" he breathed the curse with feeling—feeling he couldn't properly express in words.

Looking down on her head, he found her face hidden in his chest and feared what it meant. Now that his overpowering, driving need had been sated, he wondered where he stood in her regard. Perfect sex was one thing—they had that nailed. There was no doubt she had orgasmed on his fuck. But he'd had to tie her to a post to get her there. He wasn't sure whether he should apologize or thank her. Again, he found himself wishing he could get a hint of her feelings.

Pulling away from her a few inches, he smoothed her hair out of her eyes and sought the answer in her face, but her gaze was thoughtfully lowered. She wasn't giving anything away.

"Look at me, Martigay," he commanded with a rough grate of sound. With his hands on either side of her head, he lifted her face but still her eyes were averted downward. Finally, he followed her gaze and found it fixed on his arm—his left arm, just above his elbow where he wore her dark braid of hair, knotted below his biceps.

"Listen to me, girl. I'm keeping you. If I have to tie you to my bed, tie you to my horse, I will. But I'm keeping you."

Loosening her bindings gave him a reason to keep his arms around her and that's what he did. As her wrists were freed, he caged her, fearing she'd bolt, but she stood quietly within the circle of his arms, rubbing her wrists beneath the rope that bound her. Taking the ropes tied around her wrists, he led her to his cot. She was strangely quiet as he finished undressing. When he lay down, he pulled her down with him as he collected the ropes and knotted them off behind his back.

If she had any plans to leave him in the night, he'd know of it.

And he'd stop her.

Chapter Eighteen

"So how was he?"

Martigay sighed in the glow of the new pink dawn. "Well, let me put it this way, Pall. Before I realized it was him, when I thought it was you, I was ready to ask you—no, *beg you*—to wed me. So long as you plowed my furrow every night."

Pall smiled. "I love it when you talk agriculture."

They stood together in the small clearing where her tent had been pitched the day before. Guiding her pony's ears through the halter loops, Martigay reached back to take the saddle out of Pall's hands. "Impressed?"

He nodded, a melancholy expression in his green eyes.

"What are you thinking?"

"That the king's probably in love with you," he told her with a diffident shrug. "Only he hasn't figured it out yet."

She snorted. "Oh come on, Pall. Men like that don't fall in love."

"Men like what?"

"Men like that! Men who can have any woman they want. Men who've *had* every woman they want!" Planting a foot in Pall's locked hands, she swung herself up into the saddle. "Wanted," she corrected herself.

He grinned. "Men like me?"

She smiled at him fondly, leaning over to ruffle the straw on his head. "Yeah. Men like you."

"Oh, aye." He cleared his throat importantly. "Men like me don't fall in love…except maybe once in a lifetime. So…are you going to forgive him?"

"I don't know. Most like. I'll let you know when I get back."

He grinned up at her. "*When* you get back? You're not leaving him, then?"

"Mithra and Donar, no! The man's wearing my braid on his arm! And you *know* how I feel about sex."

He laughed. "But you mean to keep the poor man guessing. That's cold, Martigay." She lifted her chin as she smiled. "How long?"

"I'll be back before firstmeal. I'm not on duty until after that," she laughed in answer. "He can sweat a bit until then."

"Which way are you headed?"

"West should be a safe enough ride. I just talked to a scout who rode in from the west last night. He didn't see anything. I won't go far. Just give Scarface a chance to stretch his legs."

"You be careful, just the same," Pall told her.

"I'll be careful," she answered as, tossing her reins, she nudged her mount forward.

* * * * *

Dye came awake with a start, alone on his cot, clutching at the empty space beside him to find the loose ropes puddled on the blankets. His astonishment at Martigay's escape was immediately eclipsed by his fear of what it meant. Despite her obvious attraction to him, despite all they had going sexually, she had left him. Guessing she was still angry with him, he slung the tangle of rope across the tent. He was dragging his doeskins up his legs as he crossed the tent and brushed outside.

"When did the girl leave?" he asked the guard who stood outside his door. It was the same Thrall who'd carried her in.

"My Lord?"

"Martigay. How long ago did she leave?"

The guard's eyes widened. "Sir. She didn't. I mean, she hasn't. Is she not inside?"

149

Dye cursed.

Heading for the clearing where he'd last seen her horse, he found it empty. For several moments he stared blankly at the space where he wanted to see her paint.

She'd left him.

"Sir!" His guards warned him of his scout's approach. Turning, Dye found Brand weaving his mount toward him at a trot.

"Commander, the enemy is on the march. They approach from the west."

Rapidly, Dye's mind shifted gears as he turned back toward his headquarters. "West?"

Brand nodded. "They must have marched north in the night."

"How many? Where did you last see them?"

Brand answered in dismount. Together they strode toward his tent, Dye flinging orders at his two guards. "Command my lieutenants to join me. Order the men to strike and harness. Change that!" he stopped his guards before they'd turned. "Order the men to harness only, leave their tents pitched. Find my messengers and send them to me.

"Brand. Did you pass anyone on your way here?"

"Commander?"

Dye didn't look at the man. "One of my captains?"

Dye didn't see the man's cynical smile. "The one on the paint pony?"

Dye stopped and faced the man. "Did you see her?" he demanded with a voice like a knife.

Brand nodded with amusement unbecoming a king's scout. "At a distance, Commander. Heading southwest." Dye bit back the criticism that leapt to his lips, knowing Brand's first obligation was to report to his commander, rather than try to warn a single soldier at a distance. "Where was the king's captain going?" the Raith queried, and Dye resented the man's question. "Was she on a mission for you?"

"That information is…classified," Dye grated out.

"Yes, Commander." The man's response was deferential, automatic and entirely unconvincing. Just before they reached Dye's tent, Brand stopped a moment. "Commander," he said, and Dye turned impatiently to face him. "She'll be all right. The girl's very…resourceful."

"I know that as well as anyone, Brand," he said warningly.

Brand smiled at the king's anger. "As you say, Commander."

Brand followed his commander into the pavilion and Dye strapped on a leather breastplate as his lieutenants assembled in his tent, along with Davik and Warrik, to hear the scout repeat his report. There was a hard knot of anxiety in his stomach which he tried to ignore.

She was riding right into them!

"Brand, describe the country between our camp and the enemy's current position," he ordered, stalling for time. Several of his lieutenants growled, knowing without Brand's report that the land rolled gently uphill to the west.

"We have to get out of this valley," Greegor reminded everyone after Brand's report of the local geography. "The east bank is too steep for a riverside defense."

Dye nodded.

"If they're keen on the fight, we should retreat far enough to take the high ground, make them come to us, fight on our terms," Greegor put forth.

Dye nodded again. That meant pulling back to climb east out of the valley. That meant moving further away from her. *Mithra!* Dye scraped a hand through his hair.

"Get your men mounted and armed. We pull back to the south." He forced the words out of his mouth, feeling sick as he did so.

Would she be captured? How would he know? Hopefully, she'd see the Saharat before they saw her. Would she turn back if she saw them or simply detour around them and continue…to leave him. How would he know if she'd been captured, killed?

"South?" The word slipped from Greegor's mouth, a surprised question.

Dye nodded at his lieutenant. "East or west, we'll find ourselves trapped between the two Saharat forces."

"You expect the Saharat in the city to leave the walls and join the attack?" Greegor's voice was incredulous. "Leave the walls of Amdahl?"

"I wouldn't do it and neither would you, Greegor. But the Saharat love a fight. And with a mere five thousand attacking us on the west, it's the only strategy that makes sense. We'll move south, leave our tents up, camp intact. With any luck, the Saharat won't realize the camp is empty until it's too late. We'll take them on their southern flank."

Moments later, his lieutenants were moving out of his tent. "Greegor!"

Dye pulled his steel from the baldric hanging from his chair and transferred it to the belt on his hip. When he was alone with his second-in-command, he spoke. "Greegor," he said quietly. "See that my sorrel is harnessed immediately. You're in command until my return."

"Sir!"

Dye held up a hand to stop his officer's protest. "I'm asking you to cover for me Greegor. I only need a few hours. I'll be back before you've drawn the lines up south of here."

"Sir, where are you going?" When the king didn't answer, Greegor persisted. "Surely your guard, part of your guard, can accompany you."

"The horse, Greegor. Immediately."

With an angry shake of his head, Dye's officer strode from the tent, almost plowing into the huge Khal loitering just outside.

The army was already moving south in orderly ranks as Dye exited the tent. He had one foot in the stirrup when Palleden rushed toward him, dragging his mount at the end of its reins. "My Lord. Captain Martigay—"

"You're with me, soldier," he commanded. "Mount and ride."

Tearing up the rough, grassy slopes, they'd traveled no more than a league before catching sight of her upon cresting a low rise.

He saw her on the western horizon, a small dark blot streaking toward his retreating camp. With a vicious curse, Dye spurred his mount forward. Behind the girl, a long fan of black dots pursued her—what looked to be an entire unit of mounted archers. As Dye urged his horse forward, he kept his eyes on her. "Come on, Martigay," he whispered beneath his breath.

A dense cloud of arrows rose from behind to rain around her and Dye flinched, expecting to see the little horse stagger and go down under the sleeting storm of arrows. Somehow she rode through it. "Come on, Martigay," he roared.

As the flagging paint lost momentum, he watched as one of the enemy riders gained on her in sure increments. Helpless to intervene, Dye watched with sick dread as the horseman continued to creep up on her. At the same time, he was judging the distance that separated him from Martigay, calculating his own rate of advance. Sliding his sword from its sheath, his heels dug into his mount's flanks, urging more speed out of the beast as he raced forward with one intent.

To kill the man who threatened her.

After that, he had no plan. He had no plan to deal with the other fifty Saharat hurtling toward him.

A glance under his arm to locate his sergeant revealed—a hundred Khallic Northmen backing him in a tight line of thundering horseflesh, racing to catch up, with Warrik leading on his huge black destroyer. Recalling how he'd passed Warrik just outside his tent, Dye grinned as he returned his attention to the pony laboring toward him, the paint growing larger as the two horses converged to close the gap separating them.

A few more flying paces and he was past her.

The pony went by him, lungs sawing like a blacksmith's bellows, strings of lathered sweat flying from chest and flanks as its muscles bunched and stretched — the little pony struggling to keep ahead of the rain of arrows and carry his mistress to safety.

Dye's sword was swinging over the paint's rump, arriving just in time to connect with the pursuing rider. There was a resounding *thwack* and the rider's head hung in the air for an instant before it dropped and the Saharat horse barreled on, its headless baggage slumping loosely to slide out of the saddle.

In a rain of pounding hooves and blasted breaths from the horse between his legs, the king barreled headlong toward the enemy archers, dragging Warrik's Northmen behind him.

Almost too late, the enemy archers wheeled in retreat and beat their horses into a hasty departure. Warrik's Irregulars followed to cut down the stragglers as Dye wheeled his mount and kicked the beast back into a gallop. Leaning forward over the sorrel's withers, he raced to follow Martigay's track.

Mithra! He'd come within a hair of losing her.

What the fuck had he been thinking! How could he have thrust her into danger? This was his fault! No wonder the poor girl had run! He'd taken her without her knowledge, then tied her to a post and taken her again, by force. His unmanaged lust for her had driven her away from him and straight into the teeth of danger.

Pulling his horse into a canter as he splashed across the river, Dye loped through his retreating camp, looking for the paint and its rider. When he saw a small knot of soldiers clustered close to a tree, he guided his mount in that direction.

When he found her, his heart almost stopped. Reining his sorrel to a halt, he stared down at the broken beast crumpled on the ground. Slowly, his leg came over his mount's neck as he slid from his saddle and his men parted to let him through. She was on her knees, where she'd obviously been thrown when the pony had gone down. Silently, he regarded the paint's still chest before his eyes traveled to the obscene gout of blood blackening the ground beneath the pony's slack mouth.

Kneeling in the harsh, pale grass, Martigay stared at her pony. Hesitantly, her hand stretched out to touch its patterned coat. Abruptly, she stood and turned and buried her face in the nearest available surface, which happened to be the king's chest.

Dye stood frozen, arms out from his sides as his mouth opened in surprise. For several moments he stared down at Martigay's head, his expression one of frank alarm, then slowly his hands gravitated upward to case her. His arms hesitated just before locking around her, as though he feared once locked into position, they'd never come apart again. His mouth moved inexorably downward to settle on her forehead.

Slowly, he dragged his open mouth across her forehead to her temple. There his lips stopped for some time as he fought an inner battle as demanding as any wartime challenge. A groan of suppressed agony rumbled behind his lips just before his fingers were in her hair, tilting her head back as his lips smeared a path down her face to her lips. Here, he groaned again as his lips twisted into hers.

As ever, the girl fought. But fought *for* his lips this time as her head went back, neck curved, lips straining upward and sucking down his kiss like it was the only thing that would save her. Her throat was full of little whimpers—half aching yearning, the other half just plain aching.

He knew that.

He *wanted* to console her. He *needed* to hold her and know she was all right. He wanted to *kiss* her but he knew just where his kiss would lead. And he knew the only kind of solace he could offer her was inappropriate to the occasion. He'd not take her in the midst of her grief. Not at a moment of weakness. Not again. Not after she'd just left him—and for this very reason.

Dye wrenched his lips from hers. "Not like this," he moaned against the corner of her mouth. "Not like this, Martigay." Even as he spoke, his hands slid down her neck and into the top of her jerkin, causing her ties to part as his hands clutched to grip her shoulders.

Martigay's lithe body sealed against his own, her breasts against his chest — two compelling arguments threatening his resolve. Like the lock walls on the sea-to-sea channel, his hands moved out of her jerkin as his arms crushed her against him, a hand on the back of her head pulling her face into his chest — where he knew it belonged.

With his lips in her hair, Dye looked around for his men, but his remnant army had tactfully withdrawn to prepare for the move south. In the midst of a thousand men, Dye found himself standing on a kind island of privacy as Martigay's arms clamped around his waist and held him as though he was wreckage in a raging sea of sorrow.

"Come on, Martigay," he ordered gruffly. "Breathe."

Her body tensed against his a moment before he heard her long, sobbing intake. Her whole body rocked against his as though arriving at some nodding conclusion or at least agreement. When her arms loosened around his waist, he knew this was his signal to release her, but Hadi's Saints, it was hard.

As hard as his aching, throbbing dick.

Looking down on her face, he followed her gaze to the ground, where her paint lay stiff and lifeless, the pony that had carried her back to him, that had made her life possible — so that she was standing here now, warm and alive within the circle of his arms.

Faced with a situation he couldn't right, Dye battled an unfamiliar sense of helplessness as he gazed down at the little stallion. What could a man do? What could a king do? What could he do to show Martigay he shared at least some of her loss and her sorrow? He owed the horse a debt of gratitude.

At a complete loss, Dye shook his head in regret...and a glint of gold caught at the corner of his eye, saving him at the last possible instant. Immediately, his hand went into his hair as he loosened one of his three gold ribbons and pulled it free, then dropped to one knee beside the pony as he braided the bit of color into the little stallion's dark, stiff mane. Here, at least, was something she could understand.

As he finished, she knelt beside him and slipped her hand into his as she ran her other hand over the pony's coat a final time.

"Thank you," she whispered and he squeezed her hand in answer. Cutting a quick glance at her face, he let out a breath of relief to find a trace of peace in her troubled features.

The drumming sound of hooves approached, muffled in the hard grass, slowing to a canter as Pall swung out of the saddle and moved to crouch beside the crumpled beast on the ground. Eyes filled with sympathy, his gaze swung to the girl. Pulling Martigay up to stand beside him, Dye gave Pall a grim nod and then gave Martigay a gentle, separating push. As Pall stood to take her, Dye maneuvered her into his waiting arms. For an instant his eyes closed in fierce regret then he turned and moved away, ordering his final units south as Warrik's Khals splashed across the river and joined his column.

Pall lifted her chin with the side of his finger. Her quiet gaze followed the king's back. "Come on," he murmured, encouragingly. "When this is all done with, we'll get drunk. Then I'll let you shag me."

* * * * *

After joining his army in the south, Dye set about arranging his lines of attack. Escorted by Palleden, Martigay joined him not too long afterward. Her dark hair was a harsh, bruised contrast against her pale face—a face almost as white as those of his Thrallish guard.

For the next several hours, Dye was too busy to pay her any attention other than that which would assure she'd remain out of the line of fire during the upcoming battle. Where he would normally have joined his second line of cavalry, he held back and watched the conflict unfold from a distance. There was no dishonor in his action. Most leaders would hold themselves in reserve and direct a battle from a distant vantage point. Not him—not normally. But most leaders.

The two bands of Saharat had almost converged on the deserted camp before they discovered their error of judgment. In the battle that ensued, there were a few anxious moments. The armies were fairly evenly matched in numbers, but in the end, no army was equal to the elite forces of Greater Thrall—supported with superior weaponry and a mounted cavalry to put the world to shame, not to mention a never-interrupted supply line stretching from Amdahl to the coast. Dye smiled grimly. It paid to have the wealth of the civilized world at your fingertips.

The enemy gave ground in the third hour of battle and crumpled into a disorganized retreat in the fourth. The Army of Thrall followed and chased the remnant army all the way back to the city.

In the days that followed, Dye's time was fully occupied. He didn't have a spare minute. There were wounded men to be considered, funeral pyres to build and fire, as well as "gains" to be distributed. Despite the small number of losses on his side, a few of his units had to be combined and one lieutenant, along with three captains, had to be replaced. Fortunately, there were several candidates for promotion as many of his younger men had distinguished themselves in battle. Palleden was one of the men who moved up in rank.

It was a few days before he could return his attention to Martigay.

She'd left him and his army. That was the primary consideration. He had to assume she wasn't currently with him by choice, but merely a piece of battle flotsam washed ahead of the enemy's advance. This theory was supported by the fact that she hadn't searched him out privately, day or evening.

Mentally, he counted off his errors. First, he'd assigned her to the mine and subjected her to her worst nightmare—there wasn't *anywhere* on earth darker than the inside of a mine. Then he'd taken her without her permission—without her knowledge, for that matter. And after that, he'd tied her to a post and forced her.

Not a very good record, on his part. Small wonder she'd run from him.

Dye sighed. He had to further assume she might leave again whenever the opportunity would allow. She no longer had a mount—if she wanted to leave at this point, she'd be forced to go on foot. It was unlikely that she'd try to travel north to the Middle Sea on foot—it was too far. So long as she didn't have her own mount, she'd have to stay with his army.

He was tempted to leave it at that.

But this whole situation was complicated by the fact that he felt responsible for her mount's death. And not just any mount. The fastest horse in his army and equal to Hoyden's fiery line of infamous blacks. If she hadn't been running from him, her little paint wouldn't have died.

In fact, the only lingering cause he had for hope—that she wouldn't mount up and ride the moment she got a horse—was in that instant when she'd reached for his hand, after the pony's death. Dye leaned back in his chair and stared at the canvas ceiling of his tent. "Ah, fuck," he finally told the ceiling.

Chapter Nineteen

Uneasily, Dye stood beside Martigay while one of his men walked the palomino over. He'd picked out the handsomest of his four mounts and outfitted the mare in the best harness he could find amongst his men. He'd paid the soldier eight gold. It was nice work, simple and elegant. Eyebrows drawn together, he flicked a glance sideways to find her staring at the handsomely tooled saddle. Uncertainly, his eyes returned to the ruddy leather harness with its scrolling silverwork.

"I'm sorry," he said brusquely. "But you must have a mount. It was the best I could come up with." He stopped a moment, shaking his head, not daring to look at her. "I know I can't replace your little paint and I'm not trying to, Captain Martigay. But...consider the horse yours. It's...a gift."

Slanting another glance toward her, he gritted his teeth to see tears furrowing a path down her face. His fists bunched at his sides as he fought the urge to take her, hold her, drag her back to his tent and give her something to think about other than her sorrow. Breathing a curse, he turned abruptly and stalked toward his tent as he pulled both hands through the hair at his temples. Once inside, he caught the edge of his table, tossed it a good six feet and then stood glaring at the mess he'd created.

The next thing he felt were small female hands on his flanks, pressed tight against his hips and dragging downward. He shook his head as he raised his eyes to the gods. "Don't do that, Martigay. Unless you're offering more. Unless you're offering everything." Her hands stilled and his eyes closed an instant in prayer. And an instant later that prayer was answered when she dragged her hands back up his thighs.

He turned to her. "Ah, Martigay," he said. His voice was hoarse. Reaching for her, he got her face in his hands, where it belonged. Where it had always belonged. It twisted his heart to see the smudges of sorrow beneath her red-rimmed eyes. Bending his face to hers, he ran his lips across her cheeks, just below her eyelashes, where runnels of grief marked her pale face.

She leaned into him and he knew she wanted him to take her. All of her—and more than just her body—her troubled heart, her troubled soul, along with all of her difficulties and concerns. It crushed his heart to think what her surrender meant. He ached to think her sprightly soul so badly bruised, her bright, defiant spirit so beaten and crushed that she would offer it up for his taking. And would let him take her without whimper or complaint or, even more troubling, without some sly remark— so long as he would take her pain at the same time.

And because of that, because of what he knew he'd be taking, he had to ask her permission as well as her pardon before he went any further. He tipped her chin upward and made her look at him.

"I won't take you at a moment of weakness, Martigay. I won't fuck this up again. I shouldn't have done what I did to you before—in your tent after I brought you back from the mine, or here again tied to this post."

He had to hold his breath to hear her. Her response was faint but her gaze was steady as she brought her eyes to his. "You didn't do anything I didn't want you to do," she told him.

When he lifted her, she melted against him acceptingly. Accepting him and everything that would follow, should he choose to lavish his love on her with reverential devotion, or should he choose to take her like a bitch in heat. She was his at this moment, completely given for his taking.

He spread her out on his cot and opened her clothing, laying her jerkin and chemise open to reveal the fabulous swell of her breasts, slowly unfastening her leggings and sliding them down her legs along with her silk shorts and soft leather boots.

He moved smoothly, his actions carefully predictable. As he pulled his jerkin over his head, he let his eyes travel from her ankles, up the curves of her legs to linger on the dark red curls resting between her closed thighs before they followed her curves to her waist, across her belly, over her breasts and up to her face.

Her breathing was even. Her wide eyes were fixed on his, softened to a warm blue fog, filled with trust...and the vulnerability that comes with trust. He held her gaze as he untied the laces at his groin and let the stiff bow of his erection push its way out. His heart was warmed when her gaze transferred from his face down to his crotch, and he let the leggings drop to his feet as he undid the linen strap holding the blade against his inner thigh. Smiling down on her, he watched the pink tip of her tongue flick out to moisten her full lower lip and then the pearly sheen of her teeth dragging at the plump flesh caught in her bite.

It was a simple action, but seductive in its innocence. Like an impatient stallion champing at the reins, his dick jerked in response. And like an impatient stallion, he was ready for a quick mount and a hard ride. He was ready to give in to savagery and passion.

Yet, he was more than an animal. He was a man. A man with the strength to temper that passion. And he chose to take her like a man, with all of a man's simple strength possessing her body. He let her give herself into his keeping and he took her, knowing that was what she needed — the chance to give and be taken. The need to escape from herself and all the wrenching misery in her heart. The need to put herself into a man's hard, capable hands and leave herself there without thought or conflict.

Following her onto the bed with a knee nudging between her legs, he opened her and, with the weight of his long body over hers — warming and sheltering hers — he entered her in slow, gentle inches, working his way through the now familiar clenching spasms of her pussy, letting her body adapt to his presence, taking from her everything her body offered up, but only as she offered it. With his weight on his forearms, and his body against hers, he built her desire slowly with his whispering breath in her ear, followed by the drag of his lips along her jawline where he found and barely touched her lips. Slowly, he moved inside her with a steady rhythm she could depend on as her body arched slightly to bring her lips up to meet his, hovering just within touching distance.

Her breath was a warm caress on his lips, her mouth parted like the petals of an opening rose. It was difficult not to crush those lips beneath his bruising mouth, difficult not to crush her soft body with the hard, laboring thrusts his body screamed for. Sweat dampened the hair falling on his forehead as he kept up the steady pace of give and take between her legs, his gaze locked on hers as he watched the blue smoke in her eyes swirl and grow distant, unfocused. Her breathing was a soft, erratic rush, jagged against his lips, filled with small, helpless sounds.

He groaned at that whispered fray of sound.

More than anything, he wanted to pull her legs up beside his body and put his cock up against her last defense. It took every ounce of restraint and a good deal more sweat to deny himself the taking and wait for her giving. In the meantime, he dutifully delivered one quiet thrust after another while her cunt softened and grew wet around his dick, bathing his thick shaft with a woman's sweet, wet heat.

There was a change in her body underneath him, a yielding, a widening of her legs as her body started to give beneath his. A thrill of savage male excitement got between his legs as he forced his way further into the deepening opening, giving her more, knowing she was ready to take it, ready to take all that he could give, as hard as he could deliver at the back of her aching vagina. As his cock found a place at the back of her grasping sheath, the skin of his lower abdomen plowed against all the wet, soft flesh of her open sex, a rough massage of her parted lips and the clit sheltering just inside.

He heard his own rough breath, bellowing out of his lungs as he took her small, humid breaths against his lips and her knees traveled up beside his legs to his flanks then dropped flat on the bed to allow his complete penetration. Her cunt shuddered as it held his dick in a delicious grip and he continued to hammer into her as his hand slipped beneath her thigh, testing her, looking for her consent before he took both her legs over his biceps, and spread her, then rose on her.

Mithra. He loved this. Loved this fuck. Loved the tight fit of this woman's cunt wrapped around his cock, sucking at his cock head, taking his shaft in her dark, hot hold, dragging his dick toward arrival in the sweetest fuck he'd ever known.

In one still moment, he felt an exquisite tightening along his length as she started coming and he stiffened, paralyzed in an orgasmic trance of profound proportions as he joined her in climax, his dick seated at the back of her cunt, exploding against her cervix, his release pumping through his cock as he jettisoned in a blast of stunning release and all the while her body writhed and twisted on the hard, mean stake of his cock—completely taken.

His voice was hoarse by the time he finished inside her, his throat raw from the words that scraped up the strangled column of his throat to explode from his lips. Shaking his head, he watched her through the damp red strands hanging in his eyes as he growled out a final harsh animal sound of feral satisfaction—unsure of what he'd been shouting there at the end, but fairly certain he'd used the word love.

Used it several times.

Afterward, they lay together and shared low, hushed words as he watched his hand smooth over the silken contours of her body. It was almost the first time they'd talked and he had thought it would be difficult—to keep up a conversation with a woman.

But she'd talked about familiar subjects he was comfortable with. She had a number of questions about the war and his plans to take Amdahl. In fact, her interest was so keen, he might have thought she was a spy if he hadn't known otherwise.

At this intruding thought, he shifted uneasily before he swept the idea from his mind. She was a soldier, he told himself, and her interest sprang from that fact. If she was a spy, he'd kill her…after he killed himself. Either that, or he'd claim her as "spoils-of-war" and make her his slave for the rest of his life — which he would probably then spend…a slave to her pleasure.

They talked about his recent offer of amnesty to the remaining Saharat inside the city walls, and the disappointing fact that the Saharat had refused the offer. She shook her head at this, surprised the small remaining force would stubbornly refuse to surrender peacefully and settle for their lives. He explained to her that a man who wasn't likely to keep his own promises would be just as unlikely to trust another man's.

At that, she'd nodded.

He fell asleep with her body wrapped around his and woke to an empty cot. But she'd warned him that she'd ride upon waking. He'd have accompanied her, if it weren't for the guard required to trail him.

Stretching out his long, naked length, Dye rubbed absently at his morning erection and thought of Martigay.

Chapter Twenty

She was tired, she realized—dead-tired. She felt beaten, like something washed ashore after a violent storm, washed up to roll on the beach until trampled by a passing army of Clydesdales—very recently shod with iron. She felt as though she could sleep for a week, wanted to sleep for a week—her eyes turned toward the king's tent—so long as she could sleep in the king's arms.

Slipping from her mount, Martigay found a Thrall immediately at her side, yanking at her saddle, lifting it away from the palomino—one of the king's Royal Guard, ordered to assist her.

"Thank you," she told him with a wan smile and turned wearily toward Dye's tent, wondering how soon he'd be available to wrap her up in his arms.

She missed him. Missed her little pony.

As her eyes rested on the king's pavilion tent, a word wandered to the forefront of her mind, surprising her. Nothing to get excited about, she reminded herself. Men would use that word—or any other word—in return for satisfaction. Most like, it didn't mean anything. Most like, he'd not even remember it. She sighed. But man—she allowed herself a small, wan smile of satisfaction—that word sounded good on Dye's lips.

A black mare caught her eye and she winced for Dye's sake. It was Bruthinia's mount. *Poor Dye*, she thought, as she slowed to a halt before his tent.

And that was the last sympathetic thought she had for him—because, through the tent's opening, she could just see a set of very shapely, very naked legs straddling his lap.

* * * * *

"I'm not giving you up without a fight."

Dye nodded at the naked Vandal princess, pressed up against his chest. "And you've a good argument there," he told her, wryly, casting his eyes down at her brown nipples while trying to maintain his sense of humor in the midst of a very awkward situation.

He'd been thinking about Martigay, and last night— Martigay twisting beneath his body, her cunt torturing his cock in a carnal embrace—when the princess had stalked into his tent wearing a black gown closed with only two ties. In an instant, she had it open. As he stared at Bruthinia's nude body, the princess took the three steps that separated them—and was on his lap.

More than a little stunned, he leaned away from her. "What are you doing here, Bruthinia?"

"Just keeping an eye on my interests, My Lord. News from my informants was troubling enough to warrant a little further investment on my part." With these words, she let her eyes drop to her chest. At the same time, she caressed her sides lovingly as her hands slid up to cup her breasts and push them forward.

"Investment," he said.

"I'd like to offer you a little collateral, a little taste up front, in return for a small deposit on your part."

"Deposit?"

Her hands dropped to tug at his ties. "I want your silver, Dye. I want your cock inside me. I want your seed and the promise of your child."

He stood so quickly, the princess landed her delicate bottom on the ground—and none too gently. Dye stared down at the startled princess. "I can't do that," he said.

The princess worked her way onto her knees, which put her on eye level with his ties. Guessing her intent, Dye took a step backward. "I can't do that," he repeated.

She frowned at his ties, stretched tight across the thick mound of male flesh tucked inside his leggings. "What's that, then?"

"That's for…that's not for you."

The royal princess knelt before him, head tilted to one side. "Well, that's a disappointment. I hope that isn't a sample of what I might expect on my wedding night."

Dye's heart stopped. For at least two instants, it stopped. And, as he stared at the Vandal princess, the fact he'd been ignoring for so long started to come home. He was wedding this woman. This yellow-haired Vandal kneeling before him.

She was all wrong!

Everything about her was wrong! Her breasts were too small, her hips too narrow. Her smokeless blue eyes were like chips of ice. Her cold heart lacked warmth or fire. Her hair was too…yellow. She wasn't…she wasn't Martigay. She was all wrong! And he was wedding her upon a resolution at Amdahl.

* * * * *

On the other side of camp, Pall wrestled with his angry friend. "But, Martigay," he protested, his eyes flitting across the clearing to the king's tent as he locked his fingers in the palomino's halter and hoped for some sort of help from the royal pavilion. "What are you going to do? You're too ambitious to be a merchant's wife, or a merchant for that matter. You're a good soldier, Martigay."

With one hand, she palmed the tears from the sides of her face. "There's more than one army, Pall," she delivered resolutely as she swung into the saddle.

"Wha—are you mad? You're not traitor material, Martigay. Even if you were, the Saharat don't like women in their army. They don't like women, period! If the enemy doesn't catch you and burn you alive, Dye will catch you and kill you after he skins you alive! Martigay, don't do this! What in Hadi's name happened between you and the king?"

"Bruthinia happened."

"What? That little yellow-haired trollop? You can't be serious! He's only wedding her because he has to. Everyone *knows* he loves you!"

Martigay put her foot in Pall's chest and shoved. "*How?*" she shouted, gulping back the next round of tears. "*How* would everyone know that?"

Pall watched helplessly as she wheeled her mount away. "Because the only time he ever fucking *smiles*," he shouted after her, "is when he's with *you*!" Standing in the middle of camp, Pall glared first at the cloud of dust that marked Martigay's departure, then at the king's tent. "Shit!" Pall ground out. "Shit!" he delivered again in a short, violent burst as he started toward the king's tent.

"Well, that explains a lot," Pall said as he pushed into the king's tent, the two guards at the door dragging on his arms like two impotent anchors. As the Thrallish guards wrestled him, Pall stared at the nude princess kneeling before Dye, her mouth about four inches from his groin.

"Martigay just deserted your army, My Lord. Quit fucking around here and stop her before she gets herself killed."

* * * * *

Riding east through open, wooded hills, Martigay pushed the palomino to its limit and didn't slow until she thought the mare must finally rest. Even then, she loped along for another league, eventually stopping when she reached one of the many rivers that wound out of the Kelty Mountains and hurried down to the sea in a narrow rush. While her horse drank, she crouched on a rock at the water's edge and let the river's spray cool her anger.

The roar of water on rocks filled her head and she closed her eyes, letting the sound and the river fill her mind, pushing everything else aside — including those words from the king —

uttered at the moment of arrival, she reminded herself. Uttered as he had come inside her.

She almost screamed when tough fingers dug into her arm and slung her sideways to spin onto the gravelly bank.

Chest heaving, heart racketing, Martigay spun around to face the angry redhead towering before her. Outraged, she gulped in a few breaths. *"What are you doing here?* I'm not your soldier anymore," she spat out. As she said this, her eyes slid behind him, expecting to find his following guard. The brush and willow was thick next to the river and it took her a few dread instants to conclude that he was alone. His sorrel stood next to her own palomino, nose lowered to the water.

"That's why I'm here." His expression was an almost black, menacing mask of fury.

"Get out of here! I'm not coming back to your army," she insisted as she backed away from him, stumbling on the loose rock at the river's edge.

"I don't want you in my fucking army," he said in the first two steps. "I want you in my bed," he said in the next two, which put him back within grasping distance of her round, warm body. Planting his feet, he yanked her toward him and covered her lips with his.

Her feet left the ground as he picked her up, turned her and moved toward the nearest wide tree. Without breaking the kiss, he slammed her into the smooth hide of an old birch as his thumbs hooked into the top of her leggings and he yanked downward.

Twisting beneath his grasp, Martigay fought to get her lips back long enough to ask the question. "What about Bruthinia?"

"Bruthinia who?" he grated with a lust-roughened voice.

"Bruthinia—who—you're going to wed."

"How much did you see?" he growled in a threatening voice.

"Pretty much all of her," Martigay shot back. "How much did *you* see?"

"I saw the same as you," he informed her roughly. "But evidently *you* missed her fall from favor — when *I* stood up and *she* landed on her ass. She's on her way back to Tharran." His lips dragged into the corner of her mouth. "Listen. We can hammer out the details later," he rasped. "Right now I've got to get inside you before I explode inside my leggings."

The next instant, Martigay's back was sliding down the uneven surface of the tree. Dye was standing before her, back turned, steel out. A dozen men stood before him in the forest, spaced out in a rough crescent. As Martigay watched, a dozen more appeared to fill in the gaps, bows raised, arrows trained on the King of Thrall.

Chapter Twenty-One

Dye balled one large fist and heaved his shoulder forward, testing the chain pegged into the stone wall at his back. The result of this effort was nothing more than a rasping grate of sound. As his eyes went around the small, dank cell built up against the inner wall of the city, a small amount of light fought its way through the tiny barred window to fall into the chamber.

In an attempt to hide his concern, he shrugged at the girl chained opposite him. "We'll be all right," he reassured her. "They won't harm the King of Greater Thrall." Dye grunted as he threw his fist forward again, yanking on his chain. "Now I just have to convince them that's who I am."

"We'll be all right," Martigay echoed. "We'll be out of here come dusk." Slowly, she smiled at him. "You know, people might take you more seriously if you paid a little more attention to your wardrobe."

Dye stopped to stare at her. "What do you mean by that?"

"Your clothing doesn't exactly reflect your station in life. I can understand how…a person might underestimate you."

Dye grimaced as he considered his worn doeskins. "Everything happened so fast after my grandmother's death," he explained. "Clothing was the least of my concerns. I'm not a vain man," he added. "My doeskins are comfortable."

"Couldn't you at least turn in your old cloak for something…oh…something in velvet, perhaps?"

"Velvet!" Dye shot her a look meant to advise her that she shouldn't hold her breath. "Wool's warmer," he grunted, giving the chain another yank.

Martigay sighed. "I'm sorry about Bruthinia. I was tired. Otherwise I might have reacted differently."

Eyes burning with reproach, Dye gave her a curt nod. "I can't believe you were going to desert my army over that Vandal." Dye glowered at her. "That's...treason. What kind of soldier are you, anyway?"

"*Desert?* I was mad but I wasn't exactly deserting. The Saharat don't allow women in their army," she reminded him. "I was just planning to get inside the walls, help to get the gate down," she grinned, "get my next promotion."

"And exactly *how* did you plan to get *inside* the walls?"

"Pretty much the way it turned out," she admitted airily.

"You were going to let yourself be *captured*? And then what?"

Martigay shrugged. "Seduce the guards?" she suggested, looking at the heavy door across the cell.

Dye shook his head in stunned disbelief. "Seduce the—*you wouldn't*," he informed her in no uncertain terms.

"I was mad about Bruthinia," she reminded him. "Furious."

Dye stared at her.

Eventually she sighed. "I'm sorry. I know you don't care for her." She gave him a glum look. "Are you still planning to wed her?" Dye's grim expression was his only answer and Martigay sighed again. "If only you weren't so damn ambitious," she complained disconsolately. "If only you weren't so damn set on being king and ruling the entire world—as we know it."

"Set on being—" He snorted, but there was bitterness in it. "Amdahl sent a plea for help. It's part of Greater Thrall. I couldn't ignore their request for assistance. I never wanted to be king," he added in a low voice. "My sister was supposed to rule."

"Your sister? What happened?"

"Democracy."

"What?" Martigay shook her head.

"Khal is moving toward self-rule. One of the first decisions put to the vote was whether Thrall and Khal should be joined

Kingdoms. The people of Khal voted against." A little surprised light sifted into her expression. "I've a whole slew of cousins," he continued, "some more deserving to rule than I, but Grandmother felt half of them too hotheaded and the other half too easygoing. I had the dubious distinction of falling somewhere in the middle." He sighed. "I'm a farmer," he said.

"But you fought—for Khal, for the north—in the Civil War."

"Long story," he said shortly.

She raised her chained wrists. "I've nothing but time."

He smiled grimly. "My farm is in Northern Khal at the edge of the foothills, just before the land drops down to the beaches and sea. It's a big farm. It employs twenty men. The men and their families live on the grounds.

"I had no interest in the war, whatsoever, though my family favored a united Khal—so I suppose, in a way, we favored the South. My sister was wild. She got into trouble and ended up in a Southern Prison in Taranis. My younger brother went to get her out and I followed—just in time to see him die. Petra and I joined the Northern Fight with enough bitterness to wish we could wipe every Southern Flatlander off of the map.

"The conflict was ended when Petra wed Davik, the Southern Prince." Dye's chains chinked as he shrugged. "We're not very good haters."

She smiled softly. "The fact stands in your favor."

"My great-grandfather was a good hater they say."

"Morghan, The Bear of Amdahl—Tien's father. Your great-grandfather was an amazing soldier," she said, without hiding her admiration. "What kind of a soldier does a farmer make?"

Dye shrugged. "An efficient one, when he wants the conflict quickly ended so he can return to his farm. And that's where I went when the war was over. Unfortunately, Queen Tien died not long afterward and the crown fell to me. When Amdahl was attacked, Thrall had to help. This Kingdom—The Kingdom of Amdahl—was the first of Morghan's acquisitions.

King Berri left it to him on his death." Martigay nodded, familiar with this history. "But I doubt I'm much like my great-grandfather."

"Not with that red hair! Where does that come from?" His eyes filled with a teasing challenge and his hard lips formed a half smile. "What?"

"Don't you know?" he asked, shaking out his silken sheet of hair. "Can't you guess?"

Martigay gave him a blank look that lasted several instants before starting uncertainly. "It's not…Maghmarin red?" Slowly, Dye nodded. "No. That would make you Chay's—"

"Grandson."

"You're related to Chay and the Maghmarins as well as Morghan? Chay…Morghan's general?"

He nodded, pleased that he'd impressed her. "One of Chay's sons wed one of Tien's daughters. My parents."

"But" her eyes narrowed with a mean glint, "I understood the Maghmarins had a sense of humor!"

"Meaning?"

"What happened to you?"

"Thanks," Dye complained wryly.

Martigay laughed as she thought about this. "At least, I imagine it would take a sense of humor for three brothers to share a woman like Chay. Do you have any idea which of them was your grandfather?"

Dye snorted. "That's a myth—about Chay and the Maghmarin brothers. And I know exactly who my grandfather—" Dye's head came around rapidly to stare at the door just before a rattling clank sounded a warning in the keyhole.

Martigay's concerned gaze followed his. "I'm sorry about this," she apologized quickly. "This is my fault—again."

Apprehensively, Dye watched the heavy door scrape open. Without a word, an armed guard strode across the small cell while another stood in the opening. Martigay stood to meet the men while Dye got to his feet. A key loosed her chain from the wall and the guard tugged her after him toward the door.

"Take me with her," he commanded, accustomed to giving orders, but the guard ignored him. "Take me as well," Dye again ordered. "Be sensible man. I'm the King of Greater Thrall. I can make you rich."

"And I can make you dead," the guard sneered back. "Are you that anxious to join the girl against the wall?"

A cold chill of panic gripped his spine. Manacled up against the wall, helpless to stop the headlong rush of fate, he experienced an overwhelming terror he'd never faced before in his lifetime.

"Against the—take me too!" Dye roared, yanking at his chains to no effect.

The guard motioned toward the small, barred opening in the wall. "You should be able to catch most of it from that window."

"Nay!" Dye shouted.

"I'll be all right, Dye," Martigay reassured him in a rush, as the man dragged her through the doorway.

"Martigay," he roared as the door thumped closed. "Martigay!"

He tore at his chains like a madman. Then, collecting himself, he braced his feet against the wall behind him and straightened his body, trying to tear his hands through the manacles. Sweat burst from his skin to run into his eyes, while a slick flood of bright scarlet coated his hands and warmed his wrists, then dripped from his fingers. With a roar of anguish, he held his bloodied wrists before his face. His wrists and heels were stripped of skin, and still the iron shackles wouldn't pass over the big bones of his hands.

Outside the small casement, he could see the archers laughing and talking, while a number of Saharat guards prodded a long line of stumbling captives toward their end—

hapless citizens of Amdahl. In the jumble of large and small, male and female, he couldn't see Martigay, though he saw the two men who'd taken her. The archers formed a rough line, shuffling their feet, waiting for the command to draw and fire. Helplessly, he watched the bowstrings go back. Hopelessly, he heard the stinging slap of fifty bowstrings as the arrows jumped from the bows. There were screams and hoarse cries, the thudding sound of arrows slicing through flesh, the clattering sound of arrows striking the sandstone wall, followed by another round of arrows. He strained to see the wall, but could only see the archers. There was a final volley of arrows, then nothing but the archers' quiet chatter and conversation.

Dye lunged against his manacles and threw up.

* * * * *

He thought he'd not sleep again so long as he lived, and yet that must have been the first thing he did. He slept to escape to a world where Martigay still lived. He slept to escape the stinging surface of pain that seared his wrists and the deep well of agony that swamped his heart. A noise in the cell brought him unwillingly back. He didn't want to face reality.

He opened his eyes to a woman's shadowed form and thought his dreams had followed him back to wakefulness. He thought, as well, that he might be mad…and he didn't give a damn if he was. "Are you a ghost?" he queried dully.

The vision shook her head.

"I've died then, and gone to join you."

"What would you have died of?" the woman asked in Martigay's voice.

"A broken heart?" he ventured.

"People don't die of broken hearts, My Lord." She took a step toward him. "Pull yourself together, Dye. I'm a Raith."

"A Raith!" He scrambled to his knees as his eyes cut to her hair. "Henweed," he groaned. "You use henweed to color your hair red. *Why didn't you tell me?* I swear, Martigay. I'll kill you!"

A wry smile curved the lush line of her mouth. "You're welcome to try, My Lord. Death by sex would be my preference."

By now their conversation had alerted the single guard outside the door. Slowly, the door inched open to reveal the started man. But the guard was not so startled as the staring king. "Do you take *nothing* seriously?" Dye shouted at the woman in the cell.

"I answered that question, before, sir."

As the guard hurtled across the room toward Martigay, she dematerialized, stepped through the man, rematerialized with his blade in her hand and turned to slide it between his ribs. The man arched backward with a sharp scream of pain and collapsed with a rattling wheeze.

"Sex," she said succinctly. Her smoky eyes were hot on the king's volcanic blue gaze as she approached him. With a shackled wrist hooked behind her neck, he reeled her in and let her kiss him.

She had to fight her way out of his embrace. "Time to go, My Lord."

As though in a trance, he resisted the idea. Clumsily, he held her head with his chained wrists and struggled to continue the kiss he drank from her lips like the most pathetic of drunks—the kiss he needed more than escape, more than freedom, more than life.

Eventually, Martigay fought her way out of his awkward embrace and, as though suddenly awakened, Dye's eyes traveled to the door, then to the guard on the ground. "The keys!"

Martigay laughed. "Keys?" she snickered. "Where we're going, we don't need keys." Taking hold of his arms, she pulled him through his manacles, drawing in a quick breath when she saw his wrists—and his hands. Her smoke eyes were wide as they settled on the brilliance of his blue gaze.

"Dye. How…who did this to you?" She faltered as she realized what he'd done. "Mithra," she whispered. "Mithra, Dye. I'm sorry."

He stopped her with a kiss. Catching her head between the two bloody heels of his palms, he stilled her face in his grip. "It's all right, Martigay. It's all right," he told her.

She led him through the cell walls as easily as she'd drawn him through his chains. As they passed through the thick blocks of stone, a damp chill seeped into the core of his soul, penetrating him to the bone. Upon reaching the opposite side of the wall, he shivered and noticed Martigay did the same. At almost the same instant, he recognized he'd experienced a similar feeling, when standing in the river with her, shielding her from Behzad's men. With a start, he realized she must have dematerialized as she clung to him in the river. The biting cold he'd felt in his lower legs was the water rushing through his body. She'd been trying to protect him at the same time he'd sought to shield *her*.

Once into the darkening city, Dye led the way through the streets. Having visited Amdahl before, he was familiar with the layout of the city. Sneaking into a stable located near the thick wall that enclosed Amdahl, they helped themselves to a horse. While Martigay led the gelding through the fence, Dye vaulted the barrier to land beside her. "You could do that with the pony," he said, suddenly. "The path didn't have to be clear for your paint. What he couldn't jump, you took him through."

Martigay smiled at him in the darkness. "And I thought you were slow."

Dye gritted back the obvious retort. "Only when a woman requires it," he told her. "But why, then, did you let me tie you? In my tent."

She grinned. "I told you before. You didn't do anything I didn't want you to do."

For at least two instants he stood staring at her back before he roused himself and hurried to catch up. As they made their way silently back toward the walls, Dye spent the time in cynical regret—for every *instant* of wasted guilt that had dogged him since tying her up and "forcing" her. The woman was just one wicked deception following another. Still, he had to admit, there was a certain measure of relief that accompanied his wry regret.

Thankfully, they reached the stone barrier without drawing any unwanted attention. "We'd better mount here," Dye whispered upon reaching the wall. "The water's deep on the other side." Throwing himself up onto the gelding's back, he pulled Martigay up behind him.

Settling onto the horse behind him, Martigay clasped her arms around Dye's waist and pressed her lips behind his ear. "I'll get the gate," she told him, as she smacked the horse sharply through the wall. "Get back as quickly as you can."

Chapter Twenty-Two

"What!"

For a brief instant, Dye felt the warmth of Martigay's arms pass through his body—the next thing he knew, he was gasping in the cold water and his horse was swimming for the far side of the river. Frantically, he turned to search for her. She'd slid off the horse's tail upon reaching the outside of the wall. As he turned, he just caught sight of Martigay's back melting into the gray stone wall.

"Fuck!" Dye cursed at the wall after she had disappeared. As the horse dragged itself up the far bank, there was a cry on the wall. For a few more instants he stared at the blank wall while arrows began to thunk down around him like hard, heavy rain. Finally reacting, he grabbed up the reins with numb fingers, and dug his heels into the beast's flanks.

He was still cursing when he arrived back at the walls, little more than an hour later. Although the night was black, his Westerman eyes cut through the inky shadows hugging the dark stone battlement. It was clear that the gate wasn't down. His gut tightly wound with apprehension, Dye glared at the stone jetty jutting into the water from his side of the river—where the drawbridge gate should have been lowered to meet the stone quay.

"Fuck!" *Where was she?*

Sensing his tension, Dye's mount jerked its head as he reined the horse in a tight circle. "Hold your men here, out of sight," he commanded his lieutenants. "Move the cavalry to the rear and keep the horses quiet. You're in command, Lieutenant Greegor. Watch the gate," he directed, then turned to the scout at his elbow. "Brand," he ordered, "you're with me."

As his men dismounted to muffle their mounts' hooves, Dye guided his horse toward Prithan's unit. "I'm taking Captain Palleden," he told the lieutenant. The king's eyes connected with Pall's as he signaled the young soldier with a jerk of his head. Separating himself from his unit, Pall fell into step with Dye and the Raith as the king's personal guard of fifty followed, wrapped in dark cloaks and as silent as the grave.

"Did you know she was a Raith?" Dye asked his two companions in a low voice.

Pall's startled reaction answered the king's question. The horses moved forward a few more paces before Pall's slow smile caught up to his face. "That explains a lot," he whispered. "That explains the shell game." He feigned a look of outrage. "She cheated...at cheating."

"She cheated at everything," Dye agreed disconsolately, frowning at the scout.

The implacable Raith nodded at the king. "I knew. It would be hard for me not to know."

"What's that supposed to mean," Dye voiced in a low snarl.

The Raith shrugged in answer, his haughty demeanor cool and arrogant.

"Fuck me," Dye whispered vehemently, as he probed the man for emotion and discovered the man to be—a blank page. Dye could no more read his scout than he could read...Martigay.

He hadn't had much contact with Raiths, but evidently there was a lot about the strange southern race that he didn't know...and would never know—he couldn't read Raiths. Dye tore his angry gaze from the scout to glare at the walls. "She's had over an hour to open the gate. Do you think she's all right?"

Brand shook his head. "It's hard to kill a Raith...but not impossible." The Raith paused. "Obviously," he stated. "Otherwise, she'd not have lost her family the way she did. Perhaps she's still working on it." Dye nodded as his mount jostled against Pall's.

"Could Brand get us through the walls?" Pall queried.

The scout shook his head. "My Raithan blood was diluted in a human grandfather. I'm not strong enough." He settled his eyes on the king. "I'll go in alone if you order it."

Dye nodded, somehow reassured by the Raith's statement—the offer along with the fact that he wasn't *demanding* to join her inside the walls. The Raith wasn't in love with his Martigay. At the same time, it troubled him that both these men knew more about the girl than he did. That was his fault, he recognized with a pang. The time he could have spent learning about her, he'd spent keeping her at arm's length.

"We'll circle the walls as far as we can," he told the men. "Perhaps she's given up and she's out there, working her way toward us."

Abruptly, Pall reined his horse in and Dye had to wheel his mount to come back alongside his captain. The blond frowned, his eyes focused on the distant wall. "Do you see that?"

Dye flicked his gaze at the wall then back at Pall. "What is it?"

"Just a tiny glow of light…in the middle of the wall…where there shouldn't be a light."

The men stared at each other. "Her glow stone," they said together.

"Do you see it?"

Dye shook his head, unable to see the tiny speck of light that Pall could see shining on a black backdrop that didn't exist for him. "But I can see the rope," he answered softly.

* * * * *

Martigay was glad she'd thought of the rope, and taken the time to install it. Skimming along the inside of the city walls, passing through a menagerie of lesser dividing walls, she finally found a small, unguarded window large enough to admit a man. Wearing the dark cloak she'd appropriated, she'd dodged through walls and rooms, and was fortunate enough to have avoided detection. Her glow stone was tucked between her breasts, in a small net, hanging from a long loop of cord she wore around her neck. Using the cord, she tied the net holding her stone to the length of rope she'd picked up in a stable. The tiny storage room was locked when she threw the rope through the window and anchored it to a heavy stool too large to slide out through the casement. With her backup plan in place, she left the door unlocked behind her.

She was glad she'd thought of it, now that she had a clear view of the gatehouse, the number of soldiers guarding the gate, and the heavy twist of rope holding the gate up and closed. Dye's disappearance must have been discovered, she reasoned, as extra units of soldiers marched toward the walls and the men within the gatehouse worked frantically to reinforce the gate rope. From Martigay's hidden vantage point, she saw the men with a heap of leather arm shields on the floor at their feet. In an effort to protect the cable from internal attack, they were fastening the arm shields to the rope.

Taking into account the thick diameter of the tough gate rope and her own small strength, Martigay realized it was going to take some time to saw through the cable, all the while surrounded by the enemy. She could only dematerialize for as long as a person could comfortably hold his breath, at which point she had to form up again. With over a dozen men intent on taking her life, they might very well succeed. Biting her lower lip, she peered behind her. Perhaps Dye would find the rope in the darkness. And perhaps he wouldn't.

Taking several steadying breaths, she walked through the wall.

She very nearly got the damn thing cut through. As she stepped through the wall, a very startled Saharat dealt her a cleaving blow that passed clean through her, fortuitously slid between two greaves, and bit half through the toughly twined cords of the gate rope.

A long fight for life followed, Martigay only just keeping ahead of the slice and cut and jab of scimitar and dagger. Challenged with the decision of whether to cut or kill, she chose to concentrate her efforts on the rope—which did nothing to reduce the number of blades that sought her life.

The only upside was that no more than a dozen men could fit into the gatehouse to attack her. A crowd of eager candidates clamored just outside the narrow door, obviously keen to enter the fray, but unable to fit within the small gatehouse room. Eventually, recognizing the girl's determination to cut through the rope, the gatehouse guards gave up on trying to kill her and kept their steel slicing along the cable in lines parallel to the armored rope.

Chest heaving, Martigay rematerialized in a corner, gasping for breath as well as inspiration. The Captain of the Guardhouse grinned at her with a mouthful of stained teeth as she sucked for a breath.

"Give it up, girl! The gate stays closed and your army outside the walls. Push off, little Raith. Next time, tell the King of Thrall to send a man should he want a man's work done."

The screaming clamor of soldiers continued just outside the door.

"I'll have that gate down," Martigay insisted, using the back of her hand to push her damp hair out of her eyes.

The captain laughed, a harsh sound. "You, and whose army?"

At these words, there was a sudden still silence and Dye stepped through the gatehouse door. A small army of Thralls stood at his back.

"It's funny you should ask," the king grated in a cutting voice.

The room was still, the crowd of Saharat frozen in shock, staring at the weapon the king held, knowing their defeat would follow instantly on a curving edge of steel. In that breathless moment, Dye's gaze connected and locked on Martigay's.

"Here's the man you wanted for a man's work," he shouted. Swinging a long, double-edged axe in two bandaged mitts, Dye brought the gleaming curve of steel around in an arc that ended at the tautly stretched rope.

"Tell your Seiklord I accept his surrender," Dye roared—and the gate went down.

Chapter Twenty-Three

A fire crackled on the hearth but it wasn't that wrinkle of sound that woke Dye to the dawning's gray light. Languidly he stretched, thinking how pleasant it was to awaken to warm lips on his morning erection. His eyes were half-closed as he gazed down his body to find Martigay's mass of dark hair spread over his groin. The thick, dark waves stirred just before she lifted her head to give him a warm, sultry smile.

Although his army had taken the city three days earlier, those three days had been long ones—for him at least. He'd fallen into bed at the end of the each day with barely enough time for a little rough-edged sex before falling asleep with Martigay beside him. There hadn't been time for words, explanations or answers. There hadn't been time for questions. And he had a lot of them.

"Why do you hide the fact that you're a Raith?" he asked her.

Pushing herself up to sit, she curled her legs beside her as she smiled down at him. She was dressed in only the very tiniest of silk chemises. The scrap of pink fabric was barely long enough to hide the fragile peach of her nipples.

"You have to ask me that? You? Commander of Greater Thrall's Army?" She tilted her head to one side. "What was Morghan's famous maxim?" Dye nodded in agreement as she recited the famous words attributed to his great-grandfather. "When your adversary underestimates you, you've gained the element of surprise."

"Why did you hide the fact from *me*?" he asked quietly.

"My Lord! Up until recently, *you* were the *adversary*."

A reluctant grin curled his mouth at the same time that his blue eyes narrowed in stubborn disapproval.

"I...wanted to make my mark in your army," she confessed. "And I didn't want to wonder if my advancement was due only to the fact that I was a Raith and my ability to...walk through walls."

"You shouldn't have gone back in for the gates," he stated.

She considered her answer. "One of us had to fetch the army," she said finally. "One of us had to stay and open the gates. Finding ourselves inside the walls, it was too good an opportunity to throw away.

"With your night vision, you could go faster than I," she told him, "and...I didn't think I could make the ride—it was so dark." She looked at his hands, wrapped in linen. "I didn't think you could hold a set of reins, let alone a knife or sword. I didn't think you'd be able to hack through the gate rope."

"I'd have managed," he told her. "At any rate, we might have discussed it first. You needn't have kept your intentions secret, slipping off the back of that horse without warning."

She shrugged as though it was all a fine joke. "You don't need to know all my secrets, Dye."

"Secrets?" he asked without smiling. "What secrets? What other secrets to you have, Martigay?"

She smiled a teasing challenge at him. "You'll never know unless you stick around to find out."

There was no humor in his eyes or voice when he answered. "Bruthinia." He spat the word out as though he'd found a bug in his mouth. "I can't do it," he groaned. "Mithra and Donar help me, I can't do it."

Pushing himself to the edge of the bed, he left Martigay in the rumpled sheets as he padded over to the shuttered window. The cold morning was a wakeup call, a chill smack in the face as he opened the shutters and regarded the palace yard below. It was going to rain, he noted absently. The weather had been deteriorating for days—overcast, dull and threatening.

In the yard below, his army had moved aside, doubling the ranks of their tents to make room for the princess's entourage. Dye blinked down at Bruthinia's pavilion tent, flying the Vandal standards.

How could he have let it go this far? Tomorrow was the day of his wedding.

With a sigh, he closed the shutters and turned to lean against them. Dressed in only the thin scrap of silk, Martigay sat in the large gilded bed, regarding him silently. She looked good in pink, he decided, the silk chemise only one of several sets of underclothing he'd bought her upon taking the city. She looked good in the young king's bed, he thought warmly. This room had been King Berri's royal bedchamber, before he'd died and left his Kingdom to the Skraeling outlander—Morghan, Dye's great-grandfather. Shin had slept in this room, he realized— Morghan's governor to Amdahl, Tahrra's long-time advisor, and Berri's lover.

The ever-loyal Shin had never taken another lover after the young king's death. How often had Shin stood here, staring at the young king's empty bed, wishing he could undo the past? With his eyes on the woman in the king's bed, Dye shook his head as he fingered the braid just above his elbow. After several washings, the twist of hair was now nearly as blue as the ribbon it was twined with.

He'd not spend the rest of his life wishing, he decided. "Wed me, Martigay."

"Wed you!" she exclaimed, her smoke blue eyes going wide. "Why should I?"

"*Why!?* Because you *love* me."

She cocked her head at him expressively, waiting for more.

"Because I love *you*."

At that, she took a moment to smile—there was faint, fleeting triumph in it.

"I love you," he repeated, with words that felt as though they scraped over his heart on their way out of his mouth. "I love everything about you. I love the feel of you, the touch of you. I love the smell of you on my skin in the morning. I love to walk out of this bedchamber and down the corridor — through the halls — with your scent following me all day, a reminder of how I spent the night with you.

"I love the touch of you, love your pulse on my lips when I wake in the night to find my mouth pressed behind your ear. I love the feel of your breath against my lips, hot and damp just before I cover your mouth with mine. I love the sounds you make when I open your mouth with my tongue and thrust it over the rough edge of your teeth. I love the taste of your tongue, the taste of your skin, the taste of your sex when I kiss your clit and eat you into orgasm. I love the flavor of your arrival — when you spill into my mouth. Wed me, Martigay."

"What about Bruthinia?"

"You know how I feel about the princess."

Martigay's eyes were melancholy as she nodded then made a face of reluctance. "You can't do that, Dye," she said quietly. "You can't break the wedding contract. It would mean war."

Dye groaned. "Don't go all noble on me, Martigay. It doesn't suit you."

She laughed, then stopped to smile at him kindly. "You're King. King of the largest country on The Middle Sea. You can't wed a mere captain."

"I could wed a lieutenant," he smiled, lifting an eyebrow. Pushing off from the wall, he headed toward her.

She shook her head at the bedsheets, smiling soberly as she took a deep breath. "Why did you think I'd wed you?"

Dye stopped in mid-stride, staggering a bit as he backed up to lean on a table in the middle of the room. "Because you love me," he said, his tentative smile losing momentum.

"Not all weddings are love matches," she pointed out gently. "You know that as well as anyone."

It took several moments for the smile to leave his face completely. "Don't play with me, Martigay."

"I'm sorry, Dye."

"You…you were prepared to wed Pall the morning after, when you thought it was he in your tent. You said — it was the best sex you'd ever had."

"And it was," she admitted with a sigh. "And I take sex seriously, you know that. But I'd not have wed Pall any more than I'd have wed you. I'm a Raith, Dye."

"What does that mean?" His mind raced to sort the input as he tried to process what she was telling him. "That I'm not good enough for you? Leader of the largest country on the Middle Sea and I'm not good enough to wed a Raith?" He started to laugh, but it wasn't very convincing. He snorted. "So I'm to believe you don't want me. That it was just sex."

"Good sex," she interrupted.

"That you don't love me."

She didn't answer.

"That you'd never wed outside your race." He shook his head. "I'm not buying it."

She shrugged and pinned him with her eyes. "How do you think our children would turn out?"

He returned her uncompromising stare. "I think they'd be beautiful," he said quietly. "So do you."

She shook her head. "They wouldn't be Raiths."

Leaning back against the table, he grabbed the edge with his fingers and wondered where all the oxygen had gone. For the umpteenth time he wished he could sense her feelings. He was certain she was doing this for his sake, for the sake of his country, but she seemed so cool about it. So untroubled. Even cheerful.

He thought he was going to be sick.

"The ability to dematerialize would be diluted — perhaps even corrupted — when it was passed down to our children. A few generations of Raiths wedding outside of our kind and there won't *be* any more Raiths. I wouldn't mind seeing you," she offered, carefully. "After you're wed."

Dye chewed on the inside of his mouth. "So I'm not good enough to wed, but I'm good enough for the occasional fuck?"

She smiled sorrowfully. "I wouldn't want you to lose your sanity."

"I won't cheat on my wife," he announced in a soft voice of menace.

Martigay accepted this statement without comment.

He nodded, staring at the ground, still unconvinced. "Don't do this to me, Martigay," he said in a voice like splintered glass. "I'm King of Thrall." His hand fisted in the parchment on the desk to crumple several ancient maps inside his fingers. "King of the most powerful nation on the Middle Sea! *Don't tell me* I'm not good enough for you! Don't tell me you'd not wed an ordinary man!"

"You're anything but ordinary," she told him gently. "And you're a great lover, Dye. I'd not trade you for anyone…except perhaps Brand."

His head came up to meet her eyes. For a long time he searched her unflinching gaze. "You're lying," he said finally, but his emotions seethed nonetheless, seethed to the point of curdling with bitter, green, violent jealousy.

"Why do you think so?"

"Because I refuse to believe that I could have been sucked in by such a coldhearted bitch!"

"Don't be upset," she soothed.

"I'm not upset!" he answered quickly—too quickly—and he was glad, then, that she wasn't Slurian and couldn't read his feelings. "I just feel like a bit of a fool." He nodded to himself. "He doesn't love you, you know—Brand."

She made no answer.

"After all we've been through together—how can you just walk away?"

She sighed. "It isn't easy, believe me."

His nose pricked and he pressed a bandaged wrist below his nostrils as he looked at the room's huge double doors. "I won't let you go, Martigay."

Somberly, she smiled, nodding at the ground. "You can't stop me, Dye. Honor your wedding contract, My Lord."

He stared at her, his eyes an intense blue fire. A tight, painful, knotted ball of rage pulled his stomach back to grate against his spine.

"Fine," he said suddenly. "Fine, Martigay. You're right. It was just sex. I'll wed Bruthinia, if that's how you'd have it." His mouth was a thin, determined line in his face. "On one condition."

She raised her eyebrows in question.

"You be there at my wedding."

"If…that's what you want," she answered.

Her lack of regret rattled him. "Smiling. If you're there smiling during the binding ceremony, I'll go through with it. I'll wed the…pronking…Vandal princess. One woman's as good as the next, I suppose.

"And now I have things to do," he told her abruptly, grabbing up his clothing and quickly dressing, forcing his erection behind his ties as he tugged, viciously, to close his doeskins. "Let yourself out."

Once through the huge doors, he stalked down the wide, tiled corridor. Lost in a dark storm of anger, he almost ran over his sister as she stepped through a doorway into the hall. Behind her, Davik stood in the open door, half-dressed, tugging at his ties and smiling at his wife.

"What's wrong?" Petra asked after the briefest of looks at her brother. "Dye! What is it?"

Dye strode past her before he halted, his fists clenched at his sides. He turned slightly to flick a glance down the hall in the direction of the royal bedchamber. "Martigay," he said.

Petra folded her arms on her chest. "She has a right to be upset, Dye. You're wedding Bruthinia tomorrow."

Dye shook his head. "I asked her to wed me. *Her! Martigay!* She won't have me!"

"*What?* Nay, Dye, that's not possible. That woman's in love with you!"

Dye stared angrily at his sister.

"She...she...when you're with her, she can't keep her eyes off you!"

"That's not all she can't keep off me," he grated.

Petra gave him a blank look.

"It was just sex!" he exploded. "*Just sex!* Perhaps you don't understand that, Petra, but it's a concept I've no little experience with. You were right all along! The little bitch *has* no feelings!" He turned and continued on down the hall, yanking the linen bandages from his hands and flinging them away from him.

Petra watched her brother's receding back as he flung his hands into the air with a sample of the uncontained violence that made him a deadly force on the battlefield. "*It was just fucking sex!*" he shouted.

As Petra turned to her husband in the doorway, Davik ran a hand through his bed-tousled mop of hair. "Mithra!" His eyes followed Dye's back. "Is it too late to save the man?"

"I've sent for the twins. If they can get here in time, I'm hoping they'll take the throne before Dye has to wed the Vandal. Maybe that will give him the time he needs to sort this out with Martigay."

"You think one of your cousins will take the princess off his hands?"

Petra started to laugh. "You haven't met the twins," she stated.

Smiling uncertainly at his wife's laughter, Davik shook his head.

"Wedding won't be an issue anymore, after she meets Dannik and Dal. Twenty minutes alone with those two idiots and Bruthinia won't be able to tear that contract up fast enough! She'll be on her horse and heading north before the twins even start drinking."

Chapter Twenty-Four

Rain bucketed out of the sky to pour down on the King of Thrall. Slashing squalls of mean weather battered him cruelly as he stood, drenched to the skin, his flame of hair plastered to suck at the edges of his lean face. Unkind rivulets washed over his hard features as he reached up a large, rough hand, drawing it down his face and clearing the stream from his volcanic blue gaze. The nasty weather suited his mood, he decided broodingly as he stood outside his palace, at the bottom of the steps, in the yard where his army camped—his eyes on Martigay's tent.

The tight, painful knot in his stomach wouldn't permit him to eat and the vise that crushed his heart barely allowed him to breath. If this was how it felt to care for a woman, he decided, he'd be sure to avoid making that mistake again in the future.

A strong gust buffeted him from behind and lightning cracked overhead. Unbalanced, he was pushed a step forward—toward her tent. The same blast of wet wind whipped at her tent as Dye watched, volcanic eyes blazing out across the night to slash at the place where she slept. He wanted to slash at her with more than his eyes, he recognized. He wanted to hurt her as much as…

Another blast of wind hit him in the back and he stumbled forward, glaring at the tent and everything it held. The wind behind him continued and he let it push him and his anger toward the sleeping girl. Hadi help her if Brand was with her, or any other man, for that matter. Only a miracle would stop him from killing the man she slept with tonight.

His steel was out and he staggered as he allowed the gusting wind to rush him toward her, the vicious wind battering man and tent, whipping both into a frenzy. With a jerk upward, he sliced through the ties straining to hold the tent closed and protecting the girl inside. Falling to one knee, he tore at the opening and let the storm have its way with the tent's flaps as he entered the small shelter, dragging with him all the cold rage of the violent storm.

She was crouched at the tent's end, tucked into the corner, her arms wrapped around her folded legs, forehead tight against her knees.

And he realized. It was dark. For her. It was dark in the stormy, cloud-blotted night. The surly overcast weather had dogged them for days. She hadn't been able to recharge her glow stone. Drawing herself into a tight bundle, she shivered in the corner.

He almost threw himself across the tent to get to her.

Overcome with the reflexive need to protect and shelter, his throat closed to nearly choke him as he dragged her into his arms. She screamed at that first contact, pulling herself into a tighter knot. But his arms clamped around her as he pulled her into his body, shielding her from the weather that slashed in through the open tent flaps. With his hands, he soothed the chill out of her bare arms.

His throat was so tight he could barely speak. "What are you doing alone in the dark, Martigay? Why didn't you come to me?"

"Dye?" she whispered as though a prayer had been answered.

"Where's Pall?" he asked stupidly, angry that her friend wasn't there, though he would have killed the man only a moment earlier.

Martigay shuddered against his chest and he tightened his arms around her. "He's been in the city all day," she stammered. "He thought I'd be with you tonight, in the palace."

"Why didn't you come to me?" he rasped at her roughly. Her hands clung to his sopping jerkin as she raised her face in the darkness. Tears made channels on her face and his heart went out to her in the midst of his anger. "Who will hold you, Martigay?" he grated at her, his voice tight with emotion, his eyes burning. "Who will hold you in the dark when I'm wed?"

Her little body trembled in his hold. "You, Dye."

He shook his head, reaching for her lips with his at the same time. "I won't cheat on my wife, Martigay."

"I know," she shuddered out just before his lips covered hers and reduced her following words to small, whimpering complaints of passion.

She would have been content, he knew, just to lie quietly in his arms, warm in the safe harbor of his sheltering love. But—for a man—love is too tightly bound to lust. And, at the moment, his love was a growing storm of passion far too huge to deny the lust that accompanied it. Like a blasting gust of rage, it whipped into that protective harbor where foaming whitecaps flecked madly at the surging sea of his emotions.

Dye had never before in his life felt so out of control. Finally succumbing to the savage passion he'd been fighting since the day he'd met the girl, her thin silk chemise shredded in his doubled fist as he tore at her clothing, desperate to expose her naked flesh to his violating gaze, desperate to have her this one last time—have her and take her as many ways as possible before the dawn stole her from him.

The storm beat at the tent, tearing the flaps, sucking the air out of his lungs, then billowing back inside the tent to fill the small, narrow space with cold, slashing rain. At the same time, his body battered the small slip of a girl trapped beneath his weight. With a jerk of his blade, he severed the ties that held back the surging mass of his erection, skimming his doeskins down his legs and over his feet, along with his boots. With a yank, his jerkin was over his head, and without preamble or foreplay, he pushed her legs apart, put his thick cock head at her opening and entered her with one long, hard, penetrating lunge.

He plunged ahead, his hips working above her body, his dick rasping through her tight hold as her unready flesh dragged at his attack and retreat, pulling at him with an uncomfortable tightness that he ignored, so hot was he to complete the fuck and release inside the hot, dragging grip of her reluctant cunt.

She tried to reach for his lips with hers, but he jerked away from her with a ripped snarl of refusal. The storm buffeted the open tent and the rain slashed inside to sting his back and legs. With his weight on his hands, and his arms stiff, he levered his chest away from her breasts and continued to punish her with the pummeling thrust of his dick, with no thought for anything except to end the pain that built inside him, hardening his heart at the same rate that his arousal hardened the length of his shaft and turned his testes to steel.

At some point he found himself seated at the back of her cunt, his cock subject to a strange, warm fire that permeated his flesh to the thick core of his brutal length. There was an incredible, penetrating heat that warmed his shaft inside and out, followed by a crushing pressure on his length, followed by the strange, soaking heat again.

She was dematerializing on him, he realized only vaguely. The penetrating warmth he felt was when their bodies shared the same space, when she dematerialized around him. The crushing pressure on his shaft occurred when she rematerialized and his cock was forced back into her tight, narrow channel. He gritted his teeth to stop himself from flashing into her at that instant, so incredibly erotic was the sensation.

Only distantly was he aware of her legs creeping up beside his body, allowing him deeper access between her legs as she sought for a high place to hook her heels. Helping himself to the entirety of her sex, he sank himself into her depths and the tight, hot length of her cunt that wrapped around his cock like a fluttering wet flame.

"Fuck," he groaned, realizing she was creaming around his cock, her cunt loving his dick with a carnal, grasping kiss of sliding heat. "Fuck," he repeated in a falling voice of defeat, knowing he was a thrust away from spilling, knowing her soft, battered cunt was primed and ready for the rest of the fuck, begging for it to release on.

Pulling his cock, he blinked down at her face and confirmed this suspicion. Her head was tilted back and her breathing was unsteady as her body writhed and her cock-hungry pelvis lifted to find his shaft in a desperate search for completion.

With his eyebrows gathering together, he shook his head at her, his wet hair flaying his face. "Not this easily," he rasped in a low, mean whisper. "You don't come this easily, Martigay." Groaning, he got to his knees, picked her up at the hips and turned her. For an instant, he knelt behind her, hesitating on the frayed edge of control.

Then, in one swift motion, he lifted her ass to his cock and mounted her.

She cried out, her guttering voice full of stunned wonder. Falling over her, his weight on his long arms outside hers, he took her like a savage, ravaging animal, his teeth in the hair at her nape, yanking her head up and back. A rough squall of rain gusted to hit the tent in a spattering splash of harsh sound as his sweat ran from his brow to mingle with the tears he left in her hair. Like a mad, rutting stallion, he fucked her for the last time with pure male violence while she took it—all of it—like a ready, new filly, backing her ass into his groin the whole time, receiving every wicked lunge with whispered sobs of growing distress and increasing passion, pushing him to the point of madness.

"Martigay!" He choked on her name as he started to come in blinding surges that exploded through his shaft in several blistering eruptions as his body grappled with the pure racking pleasure surging through his sex. Stunned into a paralysis of gut-wrenching release, he knelt behind her as his orgasm played out and her body twisted on his, his cock brutally abused inside the sweet, hot clamp of her tight little cunt. Giving her a final hard thrust, he pulled his cock, watching the last of his silver spurt out onto the smooth skin of her rounded ass.

"Mithra, help me," he rasped with a broken voice of finality, watching her bottom writhe and jump between his splayed hands, as she bucked into her arrival like a wild, unbroken mare. Swallowing hard, he watched her as she came, orgasming without the thick, fulfilling presence of his cock to break on. When she was done, he flipped her over onto her back, wrenched her legs apart and ate at her tender, post-coital sex, swallowing down their mixed flavors. Spreading the lips of her sex, he ran his flattened tongue up through her slot, none too gently, until she orgasmed into his mouth. And screamed.

And screamed.

And screamed. Screamed that she loved him. Screamed so loudly that his whole army must know of it, except for the storm that raged around them.

He spent the rest of the night making her repeat those words, torn from the frayed column of her throat and through her ragged lips. And as the pupils of his eyes began to shrink with dawn's gray light, he was sucking on her perfect round tits, licking their reddened, ravaged nipples into hard points of exhaustion. His hand was in her pussy, stroking through her raw, swollen folds, coaxing one more orgasm out of her. And when she was close, when she was very close and running into his hands, he stopped to put his clothes back on. Watching her twist on the mat for him, he pulled his ties over the ruddy, used flesh of his cock.

Her eyes opened on his, wild with this final need and her lips parted as she begged for it. Her body was marked everywhere with the rough evidence of his love. Her nipples burned red where his teeth had scraped at her passion, her waist chapped where he'd gripped her in hard hands and clamped her against the ground as he'd worked his tongue over her clit. Her hips were deep pink, her bottom rosy where she'd been gloriously used, and used, and used again.

Her sex-tarnished skin was coated with the smell of him, the markedly male scent of his damp, straining body, as well as lavish amounts of his saliva and the sticky issue of his spewing cock. She wore the fragile film of his dried seed on her belly, a crisp, transparent second skin that clung to her own smooth flesh. Between her legs, she was filled with his silver ejaculate where he'd force-fed her cunt with cock until the throat of her vagina had choked on him and she'd throttled his dick into cock-strangling release.

He regarded her with savage satisfaction, certain that another man couldn't lie with her anytime soon without witnessing his mark on her.

"Dye," she murmured, clearly asking for more. Clearly asking for this last gift of release. Her mouth pouted up at him, not through impish design but as a result of his own rough use, her lips bruised like lush, ripe fruit—swollen and dark where he'd crushed them under his teeth.

She looked so prettily used as her lips parted for his name—and he choked back the groan that fought to voice itself.

Mithra!

Could a man love a woman any more than this?

He refused to stoop to her though he wanted that final, longing, lingering kiss. Wanted to walk away with that last sweet taste of her on his lips. Wanted to watch her body tremble through that final orgasm.

He'd offered her *everything* for the rest of her life and she'd turned it down.

She could just want it for the rest of her life, he thought savagely. He figured that was what he would pretty much be doing—*wanting it forever*. She'd rejected him and it had cut deeply. He wanted her to feel at least something of his own raging pain. Kneeling above her at the tent opening, he smiled down on her. He *forced* himself to smile. "Fuck you, Martigay," he said.

And with that, the King of Thrall ducked out of the tent into the cold, dismal dawn of his wedding day.

* * * * *

Gossip was rife that morning. For in the revealing light of a colorless dawn, more than one set of eyes had witnessed the sight of the king inside Martigay's tent, naked but for the blade strapped to his thigh, sprawled between the legs of his slender little soldier — on the morning of his wedding day.

The men of Thrall were more than a little proud, boasting that their new king had exceeded the "eight-minute rule"…at least five times in the hours between midnight and dawn. And, though only a handful of men could have witnessed the event, almost everyone had some story he was ready to swear to.

But in the various stories, the tent walls were always shaking and the harsh sounds from within implied as much pain as pleasure as the king went after the girl time and again. Other than that, it was mostly king on his knees, his hips thrusting, unmindful of how many men saw…and uncaring of how many princesses learned of it.

And later that morning, he made Captain Martigay a lieutenant. He tied the gold ribbon into her hair himself, though his fingers trembled as he did so. She deserved the promotion. She'd gotten the gates down, allowing him to retake the city in an almost bloodless victory.

So now Lieutenant Martigay wore a gold ribbon in her hair. Dye pushed out a maudlin sigh. And if that was what the ambitious little chit had aspired to when she'd bedded the king, then she'd won. But Dye didn't care that she'd won. All he cared about was the fact that he'd lost. He'd lost the sweetest fuck he'd ever known…and the only woman he'd ever loved.

And if it troubled her that her promotion came about directly as a result of her Raithan abilities…then he hoped it troubled her a great deal.

Standing outside the doors to the great hall in the Palace at Amdahl, the king shook his head. Now that the time had come, he didn't think he could look at her — Martigay. Didn't think he could look into her smiling face, knowing that smile would be her way of telling him she couldn't care less whom he spent the rest of his life with.

Madison Hayes

The rest of his *miserable* life.

His back was stiff as he pulled up his shields to protect his emotions and stepped through the door into the long hall. The princess waited for him and he joined her, taking her hand to lead her forward for the ceremony over which his sister would preside.

A figure stepped out of the crowd to stand in front of the royal couple.

It was Martigay.

She stood before them in her simple riding doeskins.

Dye's senses reeled. She still smelled of sex. Sex with him! And she was smiling, damn her. Dye took a stunned step backward as she fished inside her jerkin for something.

"Hang on," she said. "I've got it here, someplace." Then a folded piece of parchment was in her hand. She shook it out and held it up. "I'm calling in your forfeit, princess."

Somewhere in the crowd, laughter boomed out to echo in the high ceiling of the hall. From the corner of his eye, Dye saw Warrik's blond head moving above the crowd, making his way toward them. Dye didn't look at the Vandal princess, speechless beside him.

Then not so speechless. "What are you after, you common little gutter slut?"

Martigay smiled into the woman's twisted face. "I'm calling in your forfeit," she repeated. "And I'll have your wedding in payment."

The princess gasped and that's all she had time for, because Martigay stepped through the woman and came out on the other side wearing Bruthinia's red wedding gown. In her fist were her riding clothes which left the princess…stark naked.

"The king has honored his wedding contract," she announced to Bruthinia. "You have no cause for complaint against him or his country. If you have any complaint, it's a personal one—against me."

Fishing through the clothes in her hand, Martigay produced a second piece of creased parchment before the stunned princess could recover. "Warrik," she called. But he was already beside her. She grinned up at the giant blond. "I'm calling in your forfeit as well." She pointed at the naked woman. "Be a dear and take out the trash."

Grinning, Warrik moved to comply, but before he had a chance, Pall stepped between the big Khal and the Vandal princess. "Permit me, My Lord," he told Warrik. With a grunt he hefted the yellow-haired vixen onto his shoulder. "Wouldn't want you to get your hands dirty," he explained. The screaming princess went over Pall's shoulder, down the aisle, and through the door as Martigay turned to grin at Dye. Spreading her hands out, palms turned upward, she laughed. "You were right," she exclaimed, "I *do* look good in red." Slowly, the grin on her face withered and died as Martigay took in the king's expression.

"Go to Hadi's, Martigay," he said, as he turned and walked away from her.

After a brief shocked interval, wherein Martigay stared at Dye's receding back, she followed him from the hall and down the wide corridor to his room. His boots echoed in the tiled corridor while her soft slippers whispered against the cold stone floor. Silent Thralls were spaced along the walls at regular intervals, their faces impassive, their eyes following Martigay's red skirts. When she reached the door to his room, it slammed in her face with such violence it would have broken her nose if she hadn't been a Raith.

Dematerializing, Martigay stepped through the door and found Dye with his back turned and arms crossed as he stared out of the open window.

"Just let yourself in," he muttered with a voice like steel. "It's not like I can stop you."

"You're angry," she stated carefully.

His head tipped back as though searching the heavens for patience. "What did you expect, Martigay? Did you think I'd be pleased to learn you'd deceived me, once again?"

"I'm sorry," she told him. "I'm sorry I had to deceive you. But it seemed like the only solution. You asked me to wed you, and I wanted to. But you were already betrothed with a royal contract to honor. I had to deceive everyone in order to keep your honor — as well as your honesty — intact."

He answered with a quiet snort, followed by a long silence.

"When I first met you," he said, "I thought you were the boldest, most daring creature I'd ever met."

Slowly, he turned, and she saw his face. She was expecting anger. Fierce, dangerous, violent anger. She was ready for anger. She could handle anger. What she saw, instead, made her legs turn to water. She saw a man disappointed, wounded. Cheated and lied to, she saw a proud decisive man uncertain and confused for perhaps the first time in his life. Yet, despite this confusion, she saw a strong man, determined and resolved. Determined enough to walk away from wrong, if he had to. Though it might kill him.

"Most like, that was the reason for my initial attraction...to you," he continued. "But one can only be considered brave when they are in fact risking something. Their life, for instance. And now I realize that you risked nothing. You're virtually invulnerable, Martigay. You can't be harmed. You can't be stopped. You can't be touched. *I can't stop you.* You've pointed that out before. But, if I can't stop you, Martigay, I can't hold you either.

"You're...without substance, Martigay. And in more than just the physical sense. You take nothing seriously. You are never what you appear. You're a deception in every conceivable manner. You're nothing more than a clever trick at best, and a practical joke at worst.

"Aren't you?" he challenged.

But she kept her silence.

"And I'm in love with a lie! Tell me, Martigay. How can I wed a woman I can't hold, I can't trust and I can't believe in?"

Her chin came up as she met this question with her own. "If I had agreed to wed you, what would you have done?"

"I'd have wed you."

"You'd have broken your contract with the Vandals and it would have meant war." She continued without stopping. "And if I had told you of my intention to usurp the Vandal's wedding, what would you have done?"

He didn't answer.

"You would have been a party to deception. Even if the Vandals didn't think so, you would always think so. I know how much that would bother a man like you. The way it turned out, you're an honest victim of deception. And *your* honesty is more important to *you* than mine is to me," she pointed out.

"As for risk. What I did, I did to save your country from war. And what I risked was something I value far more than anything else, my life included. I risked losing you, Dye. I risked losing you, *here*. Like this."

At this point she had to stop to clear her throat. "Don't leave me," she finally tacked on the end, though she choked on the words and tears were now running down her cheeks. "My life without you would be...darkness," she said, finally settling on the worst thing she could think of.

Dye shook his head as he walked toward her. Folding her in his arms, he put his lips in the hair at her temple. "Mithra, Martigay. I have no intention of leaving you. But there's something I must be certain of before we leave this room. Before I wed you. I'll have no more lies. No more secrets. Can you promise me that?"

Lifting her head, she nodded quickly, several times.

"Then answer the next question honestly, Martigay. Do you love me?"

With a strangled sob, she buried her head in his chest as she nodded again.

Roughly, he pulled her face away from his chest and held her head in his hands. "Say it," he demanded.

"I love you, Dye."

A long desperately searing kiss followed. The sort of kiss that left them both pantingly breathless, pawing at each other with greedy desperation, pulling at clothing and pressing into one another.

Dye broke away in sudden realization, grasping Martigay by the upper arms and prying her away from his body. "Damn," he said, staring into her eyes. "Now I have to get wed with a hard-on."

Epilogue

Martigay's husband watched her face carefully, sighing as he took in her melancholy smile. Leaning against the fence, one foot resting on the bottom rung, he turned his eyes to the young colt frisking in the meadow. "Do you miss your pony?" he asked quietly.

She nodded. "Not as much as I used to."

"I love you, Martigay."

She turned warm eyes on her husband. "I love you too," she told him.

He returned his attention to the black and white colt. "He looks like his father."

"And his mother. How did you convince Bruthinia to give him up?"

"Pall had a hand in it," he explained. "Apparently, your friend is good for the princess."

"Too good," Martigay put in.

He laughed. "Rumor has it she's changed. I imagine Pall had a hand it that as well. Perhaps even both hands." He blew out a smug, philosophical sigh. "Behind every pleasant woman is a man who knows how to keep a woman content."

"Brand," she said thoughtfully.

"What?"

"Brand would make the perfect match for Bruthinia."

"I thought you liked Brand!"

Martigay reacted with surprise. "What? That conceited, smug, self-absorbed— You...you didn't actually believe I was ever *interested* in him did you?"

"Not for an instant," he lied.

Martigay whistled—two short bursts and one long. She and her husband watched as the colt's head came up and its ears sharpened. Beyond the colt, to the north, clouds dipped to touch a darkly shimmering ocean.

"Do you regret wedding a farmer?" he asked her. A bit of ocean breeze tugged at her dark blue tresses and he reached out to return the unruly strands behind her ear.

"Do you regret giving up your throne?"

Dye smiled at his wife. "Not in the least. What did you think of the new kings?"

"It's too bad they missed the wedding."

Dye shrugged. "They got there in time for the drinking. In my family, that's considered perfect timing. So—what did you think of my cousins?" he persisted.

"I love a man with a sense of humor," she answered.

"And?"

"They're two of the *finest*-looking men I've ever seen."

"And?"

"And?" she queried innocently.

"They're joined at the hip, Martigay! Did you not notice?"

Martigay nodded. "Siamese twins. Bet they're deadly in bed," she taunted him.

Dye grunted disconsolately at this expression of his wife's interest. "Do you regret giving up your commission?" he asked, to change the subject.

Martigay shrugged.

"It's a shame. You looked good in gold…but you looked better in red."

"That wedding dress fit me perfectly!"

"That wedding dress barely survived the day! It was so tight, it was coming apart at the seams—and that was before we even made the bedroom."

"*You* shouldn't have encouraged it." With an impish smile, she shrugged. "I'd not have been satisfied with lieutenant."

Dye laughed. "Ambitious little chit. You'd not have been satisfied with commander!"

Slowly, she shook her head. Knotting her fingers in the ties below his waist, she pulled him toward her. "I'm quite satisfied with *this* commander."

"I'm hardly a commander anymore," he told her. "No regrets, then?"

Martigay's saucy, trademark smile eroded as a hint of trouble shadowed her smoky eyes. Reaching for Dye's hand, she brought it to her face and turned her cheek into the large palm as her lips brushed a white scar on his thick wrist.

"I'm sorry," she confessed, "about the cell...and the manacles. About continuing to deceive you when I might have told you. I'd planned to get us out of the cell come dusk. But the guards came without warning and if they'd discovered I was a Raith at that point..." Her voice trailed away as she buried her face in his chest.

Dye gazed down on her head, surprised at the emotion with which she clung to him as well as this rare expression of devotion. She didn't normally reveal the depth of her passion for him...until she came. Thank Mithra she came often, otherwise he'd never really be certain.

"It's all right," he said gently, tilting her face upward with his fist beneath her chin. "But there'll be no more surprises, Martigay. I wed you on that condition. There'll be no more secrets between a man and his wife. Right? Right, Martigay? We're clean...aren't we?"

Sighing, she averted her eyes as she made a face of reluctance.

"Martigay!"

"I've one more confession," she admitted, "then we're clean. Remember when we were together in the mess tent? Remember the rope?"

His expression was leery. "Aye."

"I…cheated."

It took a few seconds for Dye to catch on. "You dematerialized the rope? To undo the knots?"

Guiltily, she nodded.

"And all that philosophy about loops and pairs and heads was just a bunch of crap?"

Martigay winced. "Pretty much."

Dye laughed. "And I suppose now you're going to tell me it doesn't take two to tangle at all."

Again, she nodded.

He reeled her into his body and his long, corded arms bound her body tightly against his lean, tough frame. "Pay attention, Martigay," he whispered against her ear, "because I'm about to prove you wrong."

About the Author

∞

I slung the heavy battery pack around my hips and cinched it tight – or tried to.

"Damn." Brian grabbed an awl. Leaning over me, he forged a new hole in the too-big belt.

"Any advice?" I asked him as I pulled the belt tight.

"Yeah. Don't reach for the ore cart until it starts moving, then jump on the back and immediately duck your head. The voltage in the overhead cable won't just kill you. It'll blow you apart."

That was my first day on my first job. Employed as an engineer, I've worked in an underground mine that went up— inside a mountain. I've swung over the Ohio River in a tiny cage suspended from a crane in the middle of an electrical storm. I've hung over the Hudson River at midnight in an aluminum boat— 30 foot in the air—suspended from a floating barge at the height of a blizzard, while snowplows on the bridge overhead rained slush and salt down on my shoulders. You can't do this sort of work without developing a sense of humor, and a sense of adventure.

New to publishing, I read my first romance two years ago and started writing. Both my reading and writing habits are subject to mood and I usually have several stories going at once. When I need a really good idea for a story, I clean toilets. Now there's an activity that engenders escapism.

I was surveying when I met my husband. He was my 'rod man'. While I was trying to get my crosshairs on his stadia rod, he dropped his pants and mooned me. Next thing I know, I've got the backside of paradise in my viewfinder. So I grabbed the walkie-talkie. "That's real nice," I told him, "but would you please turn around? I'd rather see the other side."

…it was love at first sight.

Madison welcomes mail from readers. You can write to her c/o Ellora's Cave Publishing at 1056 Home Avenue Akron OH 44310-3502.

Why an electronic book?

We live in the Information Age—an exciting time in the history of human civilization, in which technology rules supreme and continues to progress in leaps and bounds every minute of every day. For a multitude of reasons, more and more avid literary fans are opting to purchase e-books instead of paper books. The question from those not yet initiated into the world of electronic reading is simply: *Why?*

1. ***Price.*** An electronic title at Ellora's Cave Publishing and Cerridwen Press runs anywhere from 40% to 75% less than the cover price of the exact same title in paperback format. Why? Basic mathematics and cost. It is less expensive to publish an e-book (no paper and printing, no warehousing and shipping) than it is to publish a paperback, so the savings are passed along to the consumer.

2. ***Space.*** Running out of room in your house for your books? That is one worry you will never have with electronic books. For a low one-time c ost, you can purchase a handheld device specifically designed for e-reading. Many e-readers have large, convenient screens for viewing. Better yet, hundreds of titles can be stored within your new library—on a single microchip. There are a variety of e-readers from different manufacturers. You can also read e-books on your PC or laptop computer. (Please note that Ellora's

Cave does not endorse any specific brands. You can check our websites at www.ellorascave.com or www.cerridwenpress.com for information we make available to new consumers.)

3. *Mobility*. Because your new e-library consists of only a microchip within a small, easily transportable e-reader, your entire cache of books can be taken with you wherever you go.

4. ***Personal Viewing Preferences.*** Are the words you are currently reading too small? Too large? Too… ANNOYING? Paperback books cannot be modified according to personal preferences, but e-books can.

5. ***Instant Gratification.*** Is it the middle of the night and all the bookstores near you are closed? Are you tired of waiting days, sometimes weeks, for bookstores to ship the novels you bought? Ellora's Cave Publishing sells instantaneous downloads twenty-four hours a day, seven days a week, every day of the year. Our webstore is never closed. Our e-book delivery system is 100% automated, meaning your order is filled as soon as you pay for it.

Those are a few of the top reasons why electronic books are replacing paperbacks for many avid readers.

As always, Ellora's Cave and Cerridwen Press welcome your questions and comments. We invite you to email us at Comments@ellorascave.com or write to us directly at Ellora's Cave Publishing Inc., 1056 Home Avenue, Akron, OH 44310-3502.

THE
☥ ELLORA'S CAVE ☥
LIBRARY

Stay up to date with Ellora's Cave Titles in
Print with our Quarterly Catalog.

ELLORA'S CAVEMEN

LEGENDARY TAILS

Try an e-book for your immediate
reading pleasure or order these titles in print from

WWW.ELLORASCAVE.COM

MAKE EACH DAY MORE *EXCITING* WITH OUR

ELLORA'S
CAVEMEN
CALENDAR

WWW.ELLORASCAVE.COM

COMING TO A BOOKSTORE NEAR YOU!

ELLORA'S CAVE

Bestselling Authors Tour

UPDATES AVAILABLE AT

WWW.ELLORASCAVE.COM

Cerridwen, the Celtic Goddess of wisdom, was the muse who brought inspiration to story-tellers and those in the creative arts. Cerridwen Press encompasses the best and most innovative stories in all genres of today's fiction. Visit our site and discover the newest titles by talented authors who still get inspired - much like the ancient storytellers did, once upon a time.